SIGNIFICANT MOMENTS

By

Cecelia Frances Page

iUniverse, Inc.
New York   Bloomington

SIGNIFICANT MOMENTS

iUniverse books may be ordered through booksellers or by contacting:

iUniverse
1663 Liberty Drive
Bloomington, IN 47403
www.iuniverse.com
1-800-Authors (1-800-288-4677)

Because of the dynamic nature of the Internet, any Web addresses or links contained in this book may have changed since publication and may no longer be valid. The views expressed in this work are solely those of the author and do not necessarily reflect the views of the publisher, and the publisher hereby disclaims any responsibility for them.

ISBN: 978-1-4401-8572-4 (sc)
ISBN: 978-1-4401-8573-1 (ebook)

Printed in the United States of America

iUniverse rev. date:12/10/09

CONTENTS

PREFACE
SIGNIFICANT MOMENTS

SIGNIFICANT MOMENTS is a dynamic book of 70 short stories and articles. Some are nonfiction and others are fiction. You will read about a variety of interesting and stimulating topics. HUMAN INTEREST TOPICS are Remarkable People, Gray Hair, Survival Man, Don't Give Up, Why Settle For More?, Facing Crises, Middle East Solutions, Servers Are People, Why Do We Cry?, Why People Work, Is Television Healthy to Watch?, Endless Possibilities, Negative and Positive Situations, Dependence and Independence, Hiring and Firing Employees, Fiddle A Dee!, Why Some People Are Called Bums, Why People Are Creative, Getting Along With Relatives, Why We Think We Are Limited, Future Generations, Happenings and Soap Operas.

PHILOSOPHICAL TOPICS are Understanding Why?, Celestial Awareness, Expectations, Criterions for Living, Will Humanity Survive?, We Can Change, New Perspectives, Facing Death, Count Your Blessings and Introspections. ADVENTURE TOPICS are Jane Gwendell's Outer Space Experience, New Horizons, Voyagers, Facts About Zoos, White Cliffs, Enjoy the Caribbean Islands, Intriguing Bahama Islands, Great Britain Yesterday and Today, Look Beyond The Horizon, Wonderland

Fantasies, Floating On Icebergs, Remote Places, Fantasies And Realities and Diamond Mines.

OTHER EXCITING TOPICS are Solving Problems, Using Your Imagination, Spinning Wheels, Extrasensory Experiences, New Age Music, Playing A Harp, Rare Commodities, Different Bands, Icecream Treats, Our American Economy Today, Uses Of Glass, Our Favorite Foods, Effects of Sounds, Resolving Issues, Experiencing Fires, Uses of Rubber, Creatures In the World, Global Warming, Revolving Objects, Physical Therapy, All About Books, Selecting Textbooks and Still Life Collections.

ABOUT THE AUTHOR

Cecelia Frances Page is an author who has written 50 books. Eight books are self published. 42 books are published by iUniverse Publishers. Cecelia Frances Page has been writing poetry, short stories and research papers since the age of 19. Cecelia has a B.A. and M.A. in Education. She also focused in English, Speech, Drama and Psychology. Cecelia has published five screenplays and three, original, poetry books. Cecelia is an educator, writer, pianist, vocal soloist, piano and vocal teacher, philosopher, stageplay director, photographer and artist.

The name of Cecelia Frances Page's books published by iUniverse Publishers are: *Westward Pursuits, Opportune Times, Imagine If....., Power of Creative And Worthwhile Living, Fortunately, Certain People Make A Difference, New Perspectives, Celestial Connections, Celestial Beings From Outer Space, Awesome Episodes, Vivid Memories of Halcyon, Phenomenal Experiences, Expand Your Awareness, Adventures on Ancient Continents, Awaken to Spiritual Illumination, Seek Enlightenment Within, Brilliant Candor, Fascinating Topics, Very Worthwhile Endeavors And Circumstances, Horizons Beyond, Pathways to Spiritual Realization, Mystical Realities, Magnificent Celestial Journeys, Extraordinary Encounters, Incredible Times, Tremendous Moments, Amazing Stories and Articles, Adventurous Experiences, Extraterrestrial Civilizations on Earth, Relevant Interests, Impressionable Occurrences, Interpretations of*

Life, Tangible Realities, Remarkable World Travels, The Future Age Beyond The New Age Movement, Infinite Opportunities, Immense Possibilities, Significant Moments, Random Selections, Marvelous Reflections and more.

Cecelia Frances Page continues to write books to inspire others and to encourage her readers to be creative, productive human beings. You can order any of her books at 1-800-288-4677, Extension 5454.

ONE
REMARKABLE PEOPLE

Remarkable people are rare and unforgettable individuals who have accomplished a lot in their lives. They have developed unusual goals and objectives to live by so they can achieve remarkable results.

Some remarkable individuals are George Washington, Abraham Lincoln, Marian Anderson, Thomas Jefferson, Benjamin Franklin, Mahatma Gandhi, Nicholas Tesla, Florence Nightingale, Albert Einstein, Albert Schwitzer, Marie Currie, Alexander Graham Bell, Eleanor Roosevelt, Fredric Chopin, Winston Churchill, Helen Keller, Lord Nelson, Leif the Lucky, Mark Twain, Marco Polo, Audrey Hepburn and more.

George Washington was determined to win the war against the British who colonized the first thirteen, American colonies. Despite lack of war supplies and severe weather, George Washington led the American patriots to battle after battle until early Americans won the war against the British. George Washington became the first American president. He is known as the father of America.

Abraham Lincoln was a self educated person. He read THE BIBLE near a fireplace in his mother's cabin. He went to law libraries and studied law books when he was an adult.

He became a lawyer in Springfield, Illinois. In time, he ran for President of America. He became America's 16th President. Abraham Lincoln freed Negro slaves. He reunited all American states after the American Civil War. He is considered to be one of America's greatest presidents.

Thomas Jefferson had many talents and abilities. He played the violin. He was an excellent writer and scholar. He wrote the American Preamble and helped write the American Constitution. Thomas Jefferson formed the first American University. He became America's third president.

Marian Anderson was the first black lady to sing opera, patriotic songs and other lyrical solos in public. She was the first black lady to sing at the White House and at Abraham Lincoln Memorial. Marian Anderson made it possible for the black singers to succeed at performing for large audiences.

Benjamin Franklin became an Ambassador for America. He traveled to France and England as an American representative. Benjamin Franklin discovered electricity when he flew a kite. A metal key blazed with electric current. Benjamin Franklin was a journalist and he printed a newspaper. He wrote about political, social and religious issues. Benjamin Franklin helped to write the American Constitution. He had a strong influence as an early American leader.

Mahatma Gandhi was a lawyer in India. He went into politics in India. He became a very important political leader. He tried to free the Indian people in India from English domination. Mahatma Gandhi used nonviolent methods to free millions of Indian people. He was willing to go to jail over and over to maintain his beliefs. Eventually, the Indian people in India gained independence from Britain after their heroic war effort on behalf of Britain and the U.S.A.

Nicholas Tesla was a remarkable inventor of alternate electricity. He discovered that electricity can be produced with more light when it alternates its electric currents. Tesla drew models of rockets and airplanes. Tesla was more advanced for his time.

Florence Nightingale was a nurse. She took care of hundreds of soldiers during World War I in Europe. She established the first hospital in Europe. Soldiers called her a nightingale. They believed she was a saint because she nursed them and found better ways to clean their wounds. Florence served as a medical advisor for many years once she established the first hospital. She believed in sanitary methods to clean wounds.

Albert Einstein was a well known scientist and mathematician. He developed the famous Theory of Relativity known as M1 times M2 divided by distance. Albert Einstein played the violin with mastery. He wrote philosophical books expressing deeper thoughts. Albert Einstein presented technical lectures about mathematical theories.

Marie Curie worked with her husband. They discovered radium after years of experimentation in a lab. Radium is used in laser beams today to heal people of diseases. Albert Schwitzer gave up a comfortable life in Europe. He went to Africa as a doctor. He vaccinated many African babies, children and adults to help prevent malaria and other diseases. Albert Schwitzer lived near an African river in an African village where it was humid and hot. He played the organ. He established a hospital in this village. Albert Schwitzer lived in this primitive domain over twenty years to serve the African people who needed medical care.

Alexander Graham Bell discovered how to make the first telephone. He used cans and wires to transmit sound from one can to another can. He could hear the sound of the sender's voice through wires. Bell had to fight in court to receive credit for his telephone invention because someone stole his telephone idea. As a result of his telephone discovery millions of people can communicate many miles away by using a telephone.

Eleanor Roosevelt, wife of Franklin Roosevelt, who was an American president, became an important leader of America. She encouraged Franklin Roosevelt to become an American president even though he had polio. When Franklin became discouraged, Eleanor Roosevelt inspired him to follow through to become a strong and worthwhile American president. Eleanor Roosevelt went on to help form the United Nations. She promoted world peace and freedom of women.

Fredric Chopin, who grew up in Poland, was one of the best piano composers. He composed concertos, czernys and polonaises. Fredric Chopin toured Europe and became a concert pianist. His piano compositions became well known. Chopin gave money to free the Polish people.

Socrates was a western philosopher. He lived in Greece long before Jesus Christ existed in Israel. Socrates was a thinker. He encouraged other Greeks to think and ask questions about life. Socrates became one of the most influential and important leaders in Western society.

Winston Churchill became Prime Minister during World War II. He warned the English people that Adolph Hitler could not be trusted. Churchill told the British military to defend Great Britain from Hitler's aggressions and domination. He contacted Franklin Roosevelt to ask Americans to enter the war against Germany and Japan. As a result, after the attack on Pearl Harbor by the Japanese military, Franklin Roosevelt ordered American soldiers to enter World War II. Americans helped to defeat the Germans and Japanese regimes. Churchill continued to keep in contact with Franklin Roosevelt. Winston Churchill was a courageous and outspoken person. He promoted eventual peace for the free world which includes most of the countries of Europe, America, Canada, the South Sea islands and Australia, etc.

Helen Keller was deaf and blind. Yet, she learned to talk and eventually read and write in Braille. She was trained by a teacher on a one to one basis. Helen Keller even gave public speeches as an adult.

Lord Nelson, who was a Navy Admiral in Great Britain hundreds of years ago, was a brave and courageous person. He warned the British leaders, that Napoleon from France, could not be trusted. Nelson told everyone that Napoleon planned to dominate Europe. Lord Nelson went to sea as the leader of many British ships. He fought against Napoleon's ships and won. He was badly wounded and died from his wounds during this war against France. Without his brave actions Europe may have been defeated by Napoleon.

Leif Erickson was a Viking in ancient times from Scandinavia. He was a sailor who explored Iceland, Greenland and America. He explored at least 500 years before Christopher Columbus came to the shore of America. He developed settlements in

Iceland and Greenland. His explorations helped to pave the way to different places in the world.

Mark Twain, who lived in the 19th Century, wrote American literature. He wrote ADVENTURES OF TOM SAWYER, ADVENTURES OF HUCKLEBERRY FINN, JUMPING FROGS OF CALISTOGA COUNTY and many other stories. Mark Twain wrote for a newspaper for many years. He passed away when Haley's Comet was going passed the Earth. He became famous for his writing ability. He traveled around the world while he presented lectures about his many published writings.

Marco Polo was a traveler who went across the Middle East to China in a caravan with his father over 500 years ago. He stayed in China over twenty years and encountered dangers. He brought back silk, herbs and spices as well as fireworks to Venice, Italy. Marco Polo opened the door to the East.

Audrey Hepburn began by performing ballet. She was spotted by a drama coach, who thought she was the likely personality to play the part of Gigi in the musical entitled GIGI. Audrey continued to act in main roles in ROMAN HOLIDAY, WAR AND PEACE, SABRINA, MY FAIR LADY, DIARY OF ANNE FRANK, CHARADE, BREAKFAST AT TIFFANY'S, FUNNY FACE, THE NUN'S STORY and many more films. Audrey was a humanitarian. She volunteered to serve underprivileged children in the world. She also became a narrator at botanical gardens in Canada and the United States. She suffered during World War II in Holland. She endured and survived despite the opposition she encountered during this war. Audrey became a spy for the Holland people in order to obtain information from the Germans. She was able to give information about German plans. This was of benefit to help her people.

I have described some remarkable people who were brave, courageous and who were leaders. Many remarkable people use their abilities and talents to serve others. Some of these people have been defenders of freedom.

TWO
GRAY HAIR

Many people have gray hair as they become older. Gray hair can look distinguishing on some people. Hair fringes usually turn gray first.

Some people dye their hair different colors so as to avoid having gray hair. They do not want to be seen with gray hair because they do not want to look older. They want to look younger.

Gray hair is caused when roots inside the scalp of one's head no longer produce the regular hair color. When a person has his or her hair dyed blonde, brown, red or black he or she usually looks younger. A fancy, stylish hairdo helps to make this person more glamorous.

Having gray hair as one becomes older is a natural experience. Most observers accept gray hair on others as part of nature's plan. So, accept gray hair as part of nature's plan.

THREE
SOLVING PROBLEMS

Learning how to solve problems is important in daily life. Each problem usually has a solution. Remedies for problems can be solved logically and step by step. If problems are not solved in daily life they add up and may become bigger problems. It is wise to learn to solve each problem as soon as possible.

Problem solving requires specific methods and positive steps to resolve problems. A person must think of ways to overcome challenges and serious issues. This requires a calm, resolute approach to life.

Judy Henderson worried about her grades in college. She had difficulty passing multiple choice exams in college. During her first year of college she received three Ds, two Cs and one B. The three Ds brought her grade point average to a low C-. Judy needed to improve in taking multiple choice exams in order to raise her grades.

So, Judy decided to discuss her problem about test taking with an academic counselor. She went to see Dr. Nestor Hawkins, a college counselor. She told him she had difficulty passing tricky worded, multiple choice exams. Dr. Hawkins advised Judy to learn how to take a multiple choice exam by studying a booklet which described how to pass multiple choice exams. He handed Judy a book about how to pass multiple choice exams.

Judy thanked the academic counselor. She took the study guide booklet and left his office. She walked over to the college library and went into the reference room. She sat at a private table by herself. She began reading the study booklet. The booklet stated that a multiple choice statement which states something is always true or never true means it is not a good choice. When two statements sound similar select the statement that clearly mentions a fact about a given subject. The booklet clarified to read each multiple choice statement carefully. Then decipher the clarity of each statement. Recall information stated in college lecture notes and textbooks. Then decide the very best statement that clarifies the true and best statement. Evaluate and recognize the false statements. Recognize the very best statement.

Judy carefully studied the booklet in order to learn how to pass a multiple choice test. Judy also studied with other classmates to prepare for exams. Judy was able to answer true and false statements, essay questions and fill ins and pass this part of exams.

After studying the exam booklet Judy had a better idea of how to select the best statement in multiple choice statements. She began to pass multiple choice tests. She began to raise her grades to Bs and As. Her grade point average went up to a B average. She had solved her problem regarding how to pass multiple choice tests.

Frank Sullivan wanted to play football at his high school. However, he was short and very slender. The football coach, Jerry Nelson, told Frank that he wasn't tall enough and strong enough to play football. The coach told Frank that he could not join the football team that season.

Frank was very disappointed that he was not chosen to join the football team. Frank knew this was a problem because he wanted to play football. So, Frank decided to exercise regularly to build up his arm and leg muscles. He wore shoes that made him appear taller.

Within six months Frank became muscular. He continued to wear shoes that made him appear four inches taller than he actually was. He decided to go see the coach again so he could join the football team. Coach Jerry Nelson looked at Frank with a surprised expression. He asked, "Are you Frank Sullivan?" Frank replied, "Yes." The football coach said, "You look taller and much stronger. Have you been working out?" Frank replied, "Yes. I exercise and jog everyday."

Coach Sullivan was impressed how Frank had grown taller and that he was muscular. Frank looked at the coach with a serious expression. He asked, "Can I join the football team?" The coach replied, "Since you have developed muscles and you are taller I will try you out on the team. Be here at 3:30 p.m. tomorrow and you can try out for the team."

Frank was excited and glad Coach Sullivan finally gave him a chance to try out for the high school football team. The next afternoon Frank went to the field to try out for the football team. Coach Sullivan observed how Frank ran across the field and back with the team. Frank ran swiftly with self confidence. He caught the football which someone threw to him. He caught the football with confidence. He ran with the football as fast as he could in his special shoes. Coach Sullivan was impressed with Frank's ability to catch the football and run very swiftly with it.

When Frank had demonstrated how well he could play, Coach Sullivan spoke to Frank as soon as he returned to the coach. Jerry Sullivan smiled and said, "You played well. You can be on the football team." Frank was overjoyed. He finally had been chosen to play on the football team. He had solved his problem and he felt victorious.

FOUR
JANE GWENDELL'S OUTER SPACE EXPERIENCE

Education is very important in promoting self development and awareness of knowledge and personal, academic skills such as writing, reading and mathematics. Communication skills are vital for self growth. People who become well educated have much better jobs and to experience worthwhile opportunities about cultural enrichment and thinking processes. Educational perspectives broadens a person's outlook on life.

Jane Gwendell was raised in an educated family. Her father Glen Gwendell was a history professor and her mother, Alice Gwendell was an elementary school teacher. Jane's parents provided cultural stimulus in their home. Jane was surrounded by many interesting books and artifacts. Her parents had a television set, DVD player and VCR. Jane saw many educational videos and television programs which expanded her awareness of the world. The Gwendells enjoyed listening to a variety of music. Jane's parents read to her during her early childhood.

Jane was the youngest child in a family of four children. She learned to talk much sooner because she learned new words from her two older sisters and older brother. She began looking at picture books and listening to children's records during early childhood days.

When Jane went to school she already knew the alphabet. She had learned all of the alphabet letters and she could count to 100 when she was 5 years old. Jane was ahead of her classmates in kindergarten. She was able to read sentences because her mother had taught her to read.

Jane was at the top of her class throughout school. She became interested in many topics. She especially became interested in Astronomy, Social Studies and Music. She selected Astronomy books from the public and school library. She studied about the Cosmos. Jane especially enjoyed looking at Constellation patterns. She was fascinated in stars and planets. She wanted to become an Astronaut someday. Jane wanted to travel in spaceships into outer space to help explore our solar system.

Jane read many books about Astronomy and outer space. She read EXTRATERRESTRIAL CIVILIZATIONS ON EARTH written by Cecelia Frances Page and Steve Omar. She read DARK MISSION written by Richard C. Hoagland and Mike Bara. Jane was fascinated with these two outer space books. She learned that extraterrestrial beings have lived on Earth since very ancient times. She found that Martians lived on Mars especially when she saw photographs indicating evidence of buildings and roads on Mars.

Jane watched UFO FILES and THE UNIVERSE on The Science Channel on cable television. Evidence was shown that flying saucers have been seen by many people on Earth. She learned that stars billions of light years away will explode and send out gamma rays into the Cosmos. These gamma rays may come to our solar system within a billion years.

Jane continued to read many research books about Astronomy. She studied galaxies, nebula and constellations. She learned more about our planets in our solar system. Jane majored in Astronomy at the University of San Diego in California. She took many science courses in Astronomy. Within five years she received a B.S. in Astronomy. Jane continued to work for the M.S. in Astronomy.

Jane went to Mount Palomar which was near Vista, California south of Los Angeles. At Mount Palomar Jane witnessed a view of outer space. She was able to see stars and planets through the thick lens of the telescope.

Jane was anxious to travel in a spaceship so she could see the surface of the Earth's Moon and Mars. She hoped to be able to land on the Moon and someday on Mars to study the surface of these planets. Jane learned that Jupiter, Saturn, Neptune and Uranus are gaseous planets. She knew she would not be able to land and step on these planets.

When Jane had earned her B.S. in 2010 and her M.S. in 2012 in Astronomy she went to NASA to find out what the astronauts were doing. She applied to become an astronaut. Her application was accepted. Jane was trained to be an astronaut. She was given a spacesuit.

NASA was planning a mission to Mars. Jane was assigned for this mission. She was excited about this opportunity. She exercised and ate carefully to prepare for this mission.

Within a month Jane and six other astronauts were trained and tested in a special space module to get ready to travel into outer space. Many tests in the practice laboratory were presented. Jane learned to endure many rigorous challenges before she could go into outer space.

Finally, the big day came when Jane and the six other astronauts were expected to travel to Mars. Jane put on her astronaut suit in the NASA Station. She stepped in a large manmade rocket with six other astronauts. Many people worked in a large room to operate the rocket with electronic equipment.

Countdown began once the seven astronauts were strapped in their seats. Jane tried to relax. She took deep breaths to keep calm as the rocket lifted up and traveled into space. Jane thought about her opportunity to see and witness the surface of Mars. Jane could feel the motion of the rocket moving out of the Earth's gravitational force field. Several stages in the rocket dropped off as the rocket continued on its journey to Mars which was millions of miles away from the Earth.

The astronauts were able to move around once the NASA rocket had passed the gravitational pull. It would be a period of time before the NASA rocket would reach Mars. Jane and her astronaut companions were able to look out at space from a special window panel. They all saw the Moon as they moved near it on their journey. They were able to see the surface of the Moon.

Jane observed craters and gray rocks on the surface of the Moon. She knew the NASA rocket was not going to land on the Moon. The NASA rocket continued on its path to Mars. Jane saw large moving objects floating near the rocket. She also saw what the Earth looked like from a distance. She could see the blue oceans and continents on Earth. Clouds were surrounding parts of the Earth.

Jane noticed that there were no clouds on the Moon. She didn't see any water on the Moon. It appeared to be a lifeless place. Jane hoped to see remains of ruins on Mars. She hoped to be able to take photographs of Martian buildings and stone statues.

The NASA rocket reached Mars within several months. The astronauts prepared to land on Mars. However, a sand storm was raging on the surface of Mars. The winds on Mars were raging swiftly. June was concerned what would happen to the NASA rocket if it landed during the wind storm. She strapped herself in her sea to prepare for landing.

The NASA rocket landed on the surface of Mars in a plateau region. The winds were very swift. The astronauts would have to wait until the wind storm stopped before they could leave the rocket to explore the surface of Mars. They waited for 36 hours before the wind ceased.

Once the surface of Mars had calmed down, the astronauts decided to step out of the rocket. They put on their head gear and attached oxygen tubes so they could breathe in their helmets which were sealed carefully from Mars atmosphere. They knew they would not be able to take off their helmets. Oxygen containers were carefully strapped to their backs. Oxygen was released into their helmets so they could continue to breathe. Their astronaut suits were made to protect each of them from the temperature on Mars.

Jane was the second astronaut to step out of the NASA rocket. She followed the leader of the rocket crew, Jack Wyman. As she stepped out of the rocket she saw the surface of Mars.

The landscape was red. There were many red rocks and curving hills and crevices in the distance.

The other astronauts came out of the NASA rocket. Each astronaut carried tools to excavate and dig up rocks and soil on Mars. Jane and the others began walking on the rocky, red plateau. The sky was a reddish-gray. They could see the Earth high in the night sky. The Earth and Moon were very far away. From the Earth, Mars looks far away. Earthlings can see the reddish color even millions of miles away. The Earth appeared blue even millions of miles away.

The astronauts walked carefully in special space shoes. They observed rocks and soil. The soil appeared dusty red. They continued to explore Mars' surface. As they walked further and further across the plateau Jane noticed some buildings and a big face made of stone. They looked like the photographs collected by Richard Hoagland and Mike Bara.

Jane was excited because she recognized these Martian buildings and large stone face in the photographs. She told the leader, Jack Wyman, she wanted to go over to these objects. Jack saw the buildings and large stone face, too. He was curious about them. So, all the astronauts walked toward them cautiously. They came up to the stone face first. They were amazed that the stone face looked like a human face with two eyes, a nose and a mouth with teeth inside the mouth.

Jane took close-up photographs of the stone statue. All the astronauts walked around this enormous statue. There were no beings on Mars, however for them to meet. The astronauts examined the ruins of buildings that had been occupied long ago. Evidently, the Martians had left this area and had possibly traveled to some other places to live. The buildings were deserted. They were made of large, heavy stones put together carefully. The buildings appeared to be standing there a long time.

Jane took photographs of this deserted Martian city to take back to Earth. She also witnessed some stone pyramids which looked like pyramids in Egypt on the Earth. She wondered if the beings on Mars came to Earth to live during ancient times. She wondered if extraterrestrial beings came from Mars.

After the astronauts explored the surface of Mars they walked back to the NASA rocket. They decided to head back to

Earth while the surface of Mars was still calm. The NASA rocket was turned on and ignited. It lifted off of Mars surface and continued into outer space back in the direction of the Earth.

It took several months to return to Earth. As the NASA rocket approached Earth's atmosphere the rocket descended down to Earth's surface. All the astronauts were strapped into their seats. They felt the gravitational pull as the rocket traveled closer and closer to the ground. The rocket landed in a valley in California. Jack Wyman wired the NASA station to pickup the astronauts. The NASA Station was carefully tracking the NASA rocket before it landed back on Earth.

No one was hurt when the NASA rocket landed on the ground. This latest rocket model was more advanced so that it could land safely on the Earth.

Once the astronauts were safely back on Earth, Jane had her photographs developed right away. Her photographs were put in magazines, newspapers and science films as evidence of the Martian city and large face statue. People were amazed at the findings. Jane was pleased that she was able to explore Mars' surface and bring back evidence of Martian creations made by intelligent beings.

FIVE
NEW HORIZONS

At the brink of dawn Harrison Smith and Julia Marshall departed from their dwelling to travel beyond the horizon across the vast Pacific Ocean toward the equator. It was sunrise and the brilliant colors of yellow, pink and purple strewn across the early morning skies. Ocean currents were rippling with whitecaps. Seabirds were hovering in flocks. Some seabirds dove into the ocean to catch fish.

Harrison and Julia looked forward to their adventures as they sailed in their catamaran, 30 foot boat. They had packed food, clothing and other necessary items on their boat the day before they departed from Newport Beach, California. They planned to sail hundreds of miles across the horizon. Their journey would include a visit to many islands in the Pacific Ocean.

While Harrison and Julia sailed they wore wide rimmed hats to protect their faces from the piercing sun's rays. They didn't want to become sunburned. They wore lightweight, sportswear and tennis shoes. They were able to move around the catamaran boat easily. This boat had an upper and lower deck. The lower deck was used for storage. The upper deck was reserved for sitting and standing to view the ocean and any scenery.

SIGNIFICANT MOMENTS

Julia and Harrison had taken the necessary vaccinations for malaria, dysentery and other tropical diseases. They had packed their boat with fresh fruit and vegetables, beans, rice corn and whole grain food. She also brought five large gallon jars of spring water. They had a place to cook their food in a small kitchen on the boat.

Because Harrison and Julia left very early in the morning they had not eaten breakfast. They were sailing on their boat by 5:30 a.m. Julia prepared scrambled eggs, hash browns, toast, sliced apples and hot coffee for breakfast. Harrison and Julia sat down at a table near the kitchen to eat their breakfast. It was 7:15 a.m. and the sun had lifted above the horizon. Sunrise was over. They looked at the ocean and sky while they ate their breakfast. Harrison said, "I am really hungry. Thanks for fixing breakfast." Julia smiled and replied, "I am hungry, too. I am glad we have a kitchen on our boat."

After breakfast Julia collected the dishes and silverware to wash in the sink in the kitchen. Harrison got up and checked the sails to be sure they were properly hoisted and secured. He walked on the sun deck and felt the sun starting to warm up on the deck. He put his wide brimmed hat back on to avoid getting sunburned. He saw seagulls hovering near the boat. Some of them made gull sounds.

Julia washed the dishes in the kitchen and put them away in the kitchen cupboards. She cleaned the frying pans and put them away. She left coffee on the small stove in case Harrison wanted to drink more coffee. Julia walked out on the sundeck to see the view across the ocean. She asked Harrison,"Where are we headed for?" Harrison replied, "We are heading south toward southern Mexico. I want to go to the island of Ixaba, which is near Baja California peninsula. I have heard this is a beautiful resort island in the Pacific Ocean."

Julia thought about what Harrison said. She remarked, "I have never been to Ixaba. It sounds intriguing." Harrison answered, "I have never been there before either. I heard that the beaches are magnificent. We can sun ourselves on the beaches and go swimming in the warm ocean water." Julia responded, "I hope the ocean is warm there. I like to go swimming."

Harrison and Julia continued on their journey south toward southern Mexico at the peninsula. It would take at least two days to get there. The catamaran moved at a steady speed across the ocean. More seabirds in flocks flew overhead. It was a clear day with blue skies above. Julia decided to lay on the top deck to sun herself. Harrison navigated the boat so it would continue south along the border of Mexico. He kept an eye on the compass on the boat to be sure the boat was traveling south.

Several hours went by as Harrison and Julia journeyed south. The weather remained calm with warm sun beaming down on the boat. It became very hot and humid as they continued south. Julia stood up and went inside a small, enclosed cabin in the boat. She had been out in the sun too long and she was sunburned. She prepared lunch for Harrison and herself. She made sandwich wraps with sliced turkey, lettuce, tomato dices, cut dill pickles, avocado slices and cream cheese. She spread mustard on the corn flour wraps to add more flavor. Julia cut up boiled potatoes and made potato salad. She added mayonnaise and chopped, boiled eggs to the cut potatoes. She mixed them together to produce potato salad.

Julia served the sandwich wraps and potato salad with lemonade. Ice cubes were placed in two glasses. The lemonade was cool and refreshing with the ice cubes. Harrison and Julia ate their sandwich wraps and potato salad. They sipped their lemonade. They were enjoying their journey south.

That night the boat continued to move south. The next day Harrison and Julia would be coming to Ixaba. They slept in their deck beds under the stars. They looked up to the night sky and observed the twinkling stars and constellations. They identified the Big Dipper, the Little Dipper, the Pleiades and Orion. The Moon came out and shone brightly. It was a full Moon. The Moon moved across the night sky. It moved close to the horizon. The Moon appears very large as it was at the edge of the horizon line. Harrison and Julia observed the Moon for awhile. Then they fell asleep.

The next morning Julia and Harrison woke up at dawn. They witnessed a magnificent sunrise of bright orange, yellow, pink and some purple hues of light. This was one of the most beautiful sunrises they had ever witnessed. By midday Harrison and Julia arrived in their catamaran boat to Ixaba. They saw a silhouette of tropical palm trees against a pristine beach as they approached this scenic island. It appeared to be a paradise out of a vacation travelogue.

Harrison anchored the catamaran, 30 foot boat in the harbor. Julia and Harrison launched a rowboat in the ocean. They stepped into the rowboat and rowed to shore. They stepped on the pristine beach and walked on the pure, white sand. They looked around as they walked on this splendid beach. They saw different shells on the sand.

Julia and Harrison walked under the cluster of tropical palm trees. They enjoyed the shade under the different palm trees. Coconuts were clustered in these picturesque, tropical trees. Their palm leaves swayed in the warm breeze.

Harrison spotted an outdoor café in the distance. He spoke to Julia. He said, "Look! There is a place to sit down and get a cold drink." He pointed to the café. Julia responded. "Let's go over to the café. I need to sit down to rest." So, they walked over to the outdoor café and sat at an outdoor table. They had a wonderful view of the harbor.

The Pacific Ocean was a turquoise-blue with waves splashing to shore. There were fishing boats and regular, tourist and islander boats anchored in the harbor. Tourists were walking on the beach. There were some people sitting at other tables. They were eating and drinking at this café. They were visiting and observing the fantastic view of the harbor and beach.

Jane and Harrison sat down at one of the tables. A café waitress came to their table. She asked what they wanted to eat and drink. Harrison replied, "I will have a cold ginger ale." Julia responded, "I will have a cold ice tea." The waitress walked away from their table to go get the cold drinks.

Harrison and June looked around at the spectacular view of the ocean, beach and surrounding, tropical palm trees. They were sitting in the shade. The waitress brought the cold drinks to their table and placed them on the table for them to drink. Harrison and Julia picked up their drinks and sipped their ginger ale and ice tea. They relaxed and enjoyed being on the island of Ixaba.

Harrison and Julia decided to go swimming in the harbor. The ocean was warm. They splashed around in the water. The ocean felt just right. They went swimming for a period of time. They dried off while they sat on the beach. Then they located a car rental place and rented a car so they could travel around the island of Ixaba.

The island of Ixaba had many tall, tropical, palm trees to view as they journeyed around this enchanting, tropical island. Harrison drove the four door sedan. Julia took photographs of different views of the island as they passed by many scenic locations. It took them several hours to drive around this island.

Once Harrison and Julia were back to the same harbor they started from they decided to have dinner at a local, harbor restaurant. They sat on a terrace overlooking the scenic harbor. They ordered Mahi Mahi fish and chips. They ate cole slaw and crackers. They ordered cold drinks with this meal.

While Harrison and Julia were eating their dinner they appreciated viewing a colorful sunset of bright orange, red, yellow and pink hues near the horizon. They listened to Mexican music. Several Mexican performers played guitars and sang Mexican songs.

After dinner Julia and Harrison strolled on the beach. They walked in the water near the edge of the wet sand. They felt the rhythm of the ocean under their feet. This rhythm relaxed them. They felt in harmony and oneness with the ocean.

When it was 9:00 p.m. the sun had set. Harrison and Julia went back to their boat in their small rowboat. They slept on deck on their boat that night. The air was 80 degrees most of the night. They witnessed the stars again that night. They saw meteorites flickering across the night sky.

The next day Harrison and Julia woke up early to enjoy a brilliant sunrise over the horizon. They enjoyed seeing the bright colors of orange, yellow, pink as well as purple hues. They were uplifted when they observed this marvelous view near the horizon.

SIGNIFICANT MOMENTS

After several days and nights on Ixaba, Harrison and Julia sailed back to Newport Beach in California where they lived. They had many pleasant memories of their journey to the Pacific Ocean to Ixaba and back. They planned to take more sailing trips to experience more exciting adventures.

SIX
SURVIVAL MAN

Mark Jefferson liked to experience adventures in remote, wilderness regions. He packed camping equipment and some food to take with him on his journey. He wore camping clothes and a protective hat to keep sunshine from piercing his skin. He wore leather boots to protect his feet. He wore a warm jacket to keep warmer especially at night.

Mark was capable of climbing mountains, hills and mesas. He was a good swimmer and he was able to walk for many miles a day. He had camping skills such as a knife to cut wood. Mark knew how to create fire by rubbing two sticks together swiftly to produce heat and friction. A fire was lit in the brush.

Mark knew how to create a campfire by digging a hole. He placed cut logs in the hole. He gathered brush to put over the logs. He lit the brush first. The burning brush caused the logs to start burning. When the logs started burning Mark added new logs when they were needed.

Mark brought some cooking utensils, a metal plate, a metal bowl, metal cup, silverware, several pots, a large metal spoon, some potholders and containers of cut fruit and vegetables. He brought sacks of grain in his backpack. He carried pocket knives for emergencies.

SIGNIFICANT MOMENTS

Mark was well prepared for his wilderness excursions. He planned to trek to remote, wilderness places in the days and nights to come. He began his journey into the wilderness near Mount Herman in the U.S.A. He traveled by himself. He brought a flashlight to see in the dark.

The wilderness was quite dense with scrubs, ferns, mossy trees, wild flowers, grass and lichen. Wild animals roamed in this region. There were squirrels, wild hares, opossums, raccoons, deer, bears, red foxes, mountain lions, wolves and wolverines, rats, badgers and skunks.

Mark parked his jeep at the edge of the wilderness. He took his backpack out of his jeep and strapped it on his back. He locked his jeep and he began trekking into the wilderness in his climbing clothes. His sturdy boots were comfortable to walk on. He continued to walk through the dense wilderness. As he walked over dead limbs and through thick grass, lichen and ferns, he sensed something was following him. He kept walking and he hoped he would be safe.

Finally, Mark found out that a black bear was coming toward him from behind. Mark knew that bears can be dangerous. He decided to climb the closest tree with his backpack on. The black bear came close to Mark. He managed to climb the tall, pine tree as fast as he could. The black bear rushed over to the pine tree where Mark was. The bear raised its front legs and paws up to try to reach Mark. Mark barely escaped the black bear's paws. The bear decided to shake the pine tree gruffly. Mark held on tight to a big branch. The bear was persistent.

Mark clung to the tree branch. His backpack became very heavy and cumbersome. Mark endured the weight of his backpack. He became tired out from this sudden ordeal. He made every effort to remain in this protective tree. He pulled a thinner branch off to use to ward the black bear away. However, it stayed near the tree. It was hungry. There was a chance for the bear to catch food.

However, Mark was able to launch himself in this pine tree until it was safe enough to come down to the ground below. He waited for the bear to give up and go away. The bear attempted to climb the tree several times. Mark poked the branch at the bear after he carved a sharp pointed shape on one end of the branch with his pocket knife. Mark tried to scare the black bear away. He became weary in his attempt to discourage the big, dangerous bear.

When it became dark Mark hoped the bear would give up and go away. Every time the bear tried to approach Mark, he continued to point the sharp end of the branch at it. Mark put on his warm jacket when it was dark. The air became much cooler when it got dark. It was a moonless night. Clouds were hovering above the wilderness.

Mark wanted to go to sleep. But, because the bear was still at the base of the pine tree he had to stay awake to defend himself. Dawn finally approached. Mark heard wild animals moving around in the dense wilderness. Owls hooted in the distance. The sun came up around 6:00 a.m. Mark witnessed vivid sun rays beaming down from the sun. It began to warm up. Mark was hungry. Yet, he hesitated to take out food from his backpack because the bear was still watching him at the base of the tree.

Around 7:30 a.m. the big black bear attempted one more time to reach for Mark, who was still clinging to a high branch in the tree. Suddenly, a deer and her fawn came into view. The big bear saw the deer and her fawn. So, the bear decided to chase after the fawn. It left the spot where it had attempted to capture Mark. The bear went after the helpless fawn.

The fawn ran as fast as it could away from the dangerous, black bear. The mother deer tried to distract the bear. However, the bear continued to chase the fawn. The bear caught up with the fawn and captured it with its sharp, bear claws. It grabbed its neck with its sharp teeth and dragged the helpless fawn to the ground and killed it. The fawn became the bear's meal.

Meanwhile, Mark had observed the bear chase and kill the helpless fawn. The bear no longer pursued Mark. Mark waited for awhile before he came down from the pine tree. He had watched the hungry bear drag the fawn away out of sight.

When Mark came down from the pine tree he continued to walk through the dense wilderness. He was hungry and tired. He decided to stop to rest and eat. He sat under a big shady, oak tree. He took some fruit and bread out of his backpack. He began eating to overcome his hunger. He ate an apple and drank some bottled water. He felt better after he ate and drank water. He decided to take a nap under the shady oak tree. He fell asleep. While he was resting small forest creatures scampered by such as squirrels, wild hares and an opossum with babies on her back. Mark did not wake up because he was so tired. Several hours went by. It became much warmer.

Mark finally woke up when he felt a mosquito sting his face. He was very warm from the heat of the sun's rays. He stood up and stretched. He put his backpack back on and continued to walk toward Mount Herman. He reached the base of this mountain by midafternoon. The sun continued to move across the sky.

Mark observed an opossum mother and her six baby opossums up in a tree branch. The baby opossums were clinging to their mother's back. The mother opossum was eating some nuts from the tree.

Mount Herman had several pointed peaks. There was snow on the top of each peak. Rugged, jagged ledges could be seen on this mountain. Mark decided to wait until the next morning before climbing Mount Herman. He knew it would be dark soon. So, Mark dug a hole. He gathered some dead limbs on the ground. He gathered some twigs and brush. He rubbed two sticks together to start a fire. Once he started a fire he lit the brush and twigs. The dry limbs started to burn. When the campfire was burning Mark roasted some wieners on sticks over the fire. He used a pot to cook vegetables and potatoes to make a stew.

Once the stew was cooked Mark added seasoning. He cut up the wieners and added them to the stew. He poured the stew into a metal bowl. He sat on a log and ate his stew. This filled Mark up. He kept an eye out for wild animals who might approach his campsite. No bears approached him while he was eating. Mark kept his fire burning to discourage wild animals from approaching him.

When it was dark Mark rolled out his bedroll. He decided to lie down near the fire. The sky was still cloudy. So, he didn't see any stars. Mark thought about the big, black bear he encountered. He hoped no bears would disturb him again. He decided to go to sleep so he could rest before hiking the next day.

During the night wild animals made strange sounds. Mark heard wolves and coyotes howling in the distance. He tried to fall asleep. However, he felt uncomfortable in this wilderness. Anything could happen especially at night. Around 3:30 a.m. in the early morning Mark had fallen asleep.

Little did Mark know a pack of wolves lingered into his area. They smelled his food. They approached his campsite. Some of the wolves snarled when they saw Mark lying on the ground in his bedroll. The wolves approached Mark. He woke up suddenly because he heard their snarling sounds. He was startled by their glaring expressions. He had a gun near his bedroll. Mark carefully picked up his gun. He sat up and pointed the gun at the wolves. He knew they were very dangerous, especially in packs. As the wolves came nearer Mark aimed his gun at them. He pulled the trigger and shot the closest wolf first. It dropped to the ground bleeding. The other wolves backed off when they saw the first wolf fall to the ground. Mark continued to fire at them. The wolves ran away quickly.

Mark sat by the fire. He rekindled it to keep wild animals away. He stayed up the rest of the night to be sure he was safe near the blazing fire. The wolves didn't come back to his campsite. The next morning Mark ate fruit and bread and he finished the remainder of the stew he cooked during the night. Then he packed all of his camping gear and food in his backpack. It was time for him to climb Mount Herman. He used ropes, nails and a hammer to wedge nails into rocks along the way up this steep mountain. As he came to jagged rocks and steep ledges he pulled himself up with strong ropes which were sliding within several pulleys held by nailed stakes.

Mark continued step by step up the mountain slope. He rested along the way on narrow ledges. He looked down into the wilderness. Mark finally reached a very high slope. He was more than half way up the mountain. He stopped to rest on a ledge. He drank some water and ate a sandwich he prepared before he started climbing the mountain.

After Mark finished his sandwich and drank more water he continued his climb up the mountain. He continued to pull himself up with ropes moving through pulleys. He finally reached the highest slope on the mountain. He looked at a panoramic view of the valley below. The view was spectacular. Mark took some photographs of the valley below. He rested at the top. It was midday.

Mark decided to descend down the mountain by 2:00 p.m. He used his ropes to help him move down the slope. He hoisted each rope carefully and came down slowly. The metal stakes were used to steady his ropes. He finally was able to reach the bottom of the last slope.

Mark made it safely down the mountain. He was relieved to be on the ground again. He needed to rest from the long and challenging climb. He was relieved to be safe on the ground again.

Mark sat under another shady tree to rest before he left this region. Once he rested for awhile he stood up and walked through the wilderness to his car. He got into his car and drove back to his home. He thought about his adventures in the wilderness. He had taken photographs along the way. He had interesting memories about his wilderness excursion. He was able to survive in the wilderness despite many dangers and challenges.

SEVEN
DON'T GIVE UP

When life becomes more than a challenge and you feel defeated you need to reflect within to cultivate inner strength and self direction. Your ability to focus on God, in order to develop the will to accomplish your goals and aspirations, is the key to real understanding and victory. Look within to seek the truth and be willing to listen to your inner voice of your higher self. You will be able to seek inner truth and spiritual guidance.

Emily Wilkins was a shy and insecure person. Her life had become a challenge with many defeats and problems. She didn't know which way to turn. She was discouraged and despondent. Her problems mounted up. She began to lose her physical health. She lost her job. Then she was in an automobile accident. Her car was demolished. So, she was without a car.

With all these calamities Emily felt like giving up. She felt her life had come to a stand-still. She wished she was dead so she wouldn't have to face her present situation. Day after day she felt depressed and lost because she didn't know how to resolve problems.

Then, one day Emily was sitting in the public park in the town she lived in. She had walked into this verdant, green setting mid-morning. She came to a bench and sat down to rest. While she was resting on the bench she continued to worry about her present predicament.

Around 11:45 a.m. a middle-aged man walked by where Emily was sitting on a bench. He sat down on the same bench. He notified Emily, who was middle aged, on the bench. Emily remained silent. She knew this middle-aged man was a stranger. He looked over at Emily and noticed that she seemed down-hearted. He decided to speak to Emily.

The middle-aged stranger continued to walk closer to the bench Emily was sitting on. He sat down on the same bench and looked at Emily. He decided to speak to Emily. Harry said, "Hello. It is a beautiful day. My name is Harry. Do you come to the park often?" Emily hesitated to speak to the stranger. Harry spoke again. He said, "I like to come here to relax and to watch ducks and geese in the pond over there." Harry pointed to the pond at ducks and geese.

Emily still remained silent. She looked over to the ducks and geese floating in the deep blue water of the nearby pond. Emily still looked despondent and disturbed. Finally she began crying. Harry asked, "What's wrong? Why are you crying.?" Emily decided to reveal her stressful feelings. She said, "Everything has gone wrong in my life! I have lost my husband, my job and my home! I wish I was dead!"

Harry looked concerned about Emily's stressful reaction about what had happened in her life. Harry sat closer to Emily and said, "I understand how you feel. I have lost loved ones. I broke my leg about a year ago. I was laid off because I couldn't work while my leg was broken." Emily looked at Harry. She was still crying. Harry continued to reveal more about his problems.

Harry said, "I have had to move to government housing into a one bedroom studio apartment. It is very small. I used to live in a comfortable, three bedroom house. I have to be careful how much I spend on food. Food has become much more expensive." Harry realized he had been focusing on his problems. He noticed Emily was still crying. "I want to help you. I have had tragic experiences. I didn't give up. I prayed to God for guidance and strength to go on. You can lick your problems if you are willing to try. It is up to you to try to overcome your problems. Focus on positive moments in your life. Realize that you can overcome most problems if you try."

Emily stopped crying. She stared at Harry. She thought about what he said. She asked, "Will you be here again tomorrow?" Harry smiled and replied," I usually come here every day. I haven't seen you in this park before." Emily answered, "I haven't been here before." Harry responded, "I will be in this park at around 11 a.m. tomorrow morning. I hope you come back to this park tomorrow morning. I would like to see you again."

Emily looked out at Harry with puzzlement. She wondered why he wanted to see her again. She remained silent. Harry stood up from the park bench. He said, "I must go now. I hope I will see you tomorrow morning. Good-bye." Harry walked away and went down a pathway in the park. He eventually disappeared out of sight. Emily watched him walk away. She thought about his advice. He had clarified that he had faced challenges in the past.

Emily eventually left the park and she went to a food bank to receive some free food. She was broke because she had lost her job. She collected food stamps and received some welfare money. The welfare money was only $425 a month. Emily had to use this small amount of money to pay her bills. She was unable to pay all her living expenses. She was unable to pay all her rent. She was evicted from her one bedroom apartment. She was forced to go to a shelter to live. She lived with thirty other, homeless people. Thirty beds were lined up in one large room. Emily had no privacy. She slept on a single bed near other homeless strangers.

Emily was concerned about her safety and comfort. At night she had to bundle up in bed because the large room was cold. She received one free meal a day downtown at a church. She had to buy food for her other meals. She went to local grocery stores to buy fruit, nuts and cold drinks. She depended on the free meal at the church to be her main meal.

Emily decided to go back to the same park the next morning. She thought more about what Harry said to her that day at the park bench. She hoped to see him again. The next morning Emily got up and dressed in a colorful pantsuit which she had pursued at the local Goodwill Store. She combed her brown hair. Emily had blue eyes. She put on her best shoes which matched her red and yellow pantsuit. Emily looked quite attractive in this outfit. Even though her health had declined she had no wrinkles in her forehead. Emily put on some pink lipstick to add more color to her face.

There were some apples and nuts in a bag which Emily had bought at the nearby store. She sat on her bed in the large room and ate two apples. Then she munched on some nuts. She was satisfied once she had eaten her breakfast. Then Emily decided to go outdoors in the sunshine to walk over to the park. It was around 9:30 a.m. when she arrived at the park. She sat on the same bench she had sat on the day before.

Emily waited for Harry to arrive in the park. She looked around and she noticed other women, children and some men walking around in the park. Children were playing on play equipment in the park. Mothers were watching their children as they played. Some people were lying down on the grass. Some boys and girls were throwing balls back and forth.

Time went by as Emily waited on the park bench. She wore a wristwatch which she had for several years. At approximately 10:47 a.m. Harry appeared in the park. He's walked over to Emily and greeted her. Harry said, "Hello. I am glad you decided to come back today." Harry sat down on the bench near Emily. Emily said, "Hi."

Harry smiled warmly at Emily. He noticed her red and yellow pantsuit and matching shoes and red cardigan sweater. Harry said, "You look nice. How are you doing today?" Emily decided to open up. She knew Harry had reached out to help her the day before. Emily said, "I'm feeling a little better today. I thought about what you said yesterday." Harry smiled and replied, "I remember telling you not to give up. I went through a rough time when my wife died. I thought the world had come to an end. It took me some time to readjust to being alone." Emily began to feel more relaxed. Harry had revealed that he had gone through a rough time in his life. She began to realize that he didn't give up because of this difficult time in his life

Harry continued, "I have had other challenges. I fell down and broke my leg while I was at work one day. Because of this accident I was laid off from my job because I was unable to work as a carpenter until my leg healed. I had to collect unemployment for six months.

Emily looked at Harry intently. He had revealed his problems to her. She said, "Are you working again?" Harry replied, "The job market is very slow right now. I have been looking for another job. I'm waiting to hear from the employment agency." Emily responded, "I'm still not working. I'm living off of welfare." Harry replied, "If you are willing to work you may be able to find a job doing something. You could look after an elderly person or baby-sit for a family. Housekeeping jobs are available."

Emily frowned and looked despondent. She remained silent. Harry looked at her with concern. He asked, "What is your name?" Emily finally responded. She said, "I don't feel well enough to work. I guess I can survive if I live very frugally. I receive one free meal a day. I have a place to live."

Harry said, "Maybe you will feel better soon. Sunshine is good for you. Have you been to see a doctor for a check up?" Emily replied, "I can't afford to go to a doctor. It costs too much! I receive very little money to live on." Harry answered, "I understand how it is. Doctors are very expensive to go to for help. I hope you are eating well." Emily replied, "I eat fruit, nuts, a salad and some beans. The meal I have at lunch is pretty good.

Harry asked, "Where do you have lunch?" Emily responded, "There is a church nearby where a free, hot meal is served every day." Emily looked at her wristwatch. She said, "Lunch is served at 11:30 a.m. Would you like to join me for lunch at the church?"

Harry's eyes lit up. He said, "Sure." Emily said, "It is 11.15 a.m. right now. We'd better walk over now so that now so that we will have a place at one of the tables. The food is served immediately at 11.30 a.m."

Emily and Harry got up from the park bench. Harry followed Emily to the local church which was several blocks away. When they reached the church they sat at one of the tables. Servers came out and served a hot meal of meatballs and spaghetti, cole slaw, toasted bread, sliced fruit and hot coffee. Harry and Emily visited while they ate. Emily was glad to become acquainted with Harry. She felt safe and comfortable with him. She felt she had another chance to make friends and to enjoy his company. After lunch Emily and Harry walked around the town and looked in the shops.

Emily continued to meet Harry regularly to stroll on the beach and walk in the park. Harry prepared meals at his apartment for Emily. In time Emily began to improve in her health. She went to live with Harry. She found a job as a housekeeper. Harry finally went back to work as a carpenter. Harry and Emily became very good friends. They had fallen in love with each other. Emily had learned not to give up.

EIGHT
USING YOUR IMAGINATION

We can use our imagination to do about anything we want to do. There are many opportunities to be creative. The ability to use one's imagination can be developed. Creative thoughts can flow through our mind. People who use their imagination can become writers, painters, sculptors, musicians, architects and worthwhile, productive businessmen and businesswomen.

Imaginative individuals become thinkers, inventors and even important leaders. Fashion designers use their imagination. Poets use descriptive words and word images to convey creative thoughts. Composers discover new melodies and instrumental music. Even cooks use their imagination in order to prepare new recipes so they can serve new dishes of food.

Cheryl Ann Martin was a creative person while she was growing up. She used her imagination to design clothes. She made new clothes for her dolls when she was ten years old. She created clothing patterns and she learned to make doll dresses, blouses, pants and jackets. She drew different designs which she used to make clothes.

Cheryl selected Home Economics as her major in high school. She learned to cook a variety of recipes. She experimented and learned to create a variety of original casserole dishes, beautiful cakes and cupcakes and fruit dishes. Cheryl continued to learn to sew adult and teenage dresses, pantsuits, sweaters, jackets and coats. She became an excellent seamstress. She eventually went to work for a fashion designer's firm. Cheryl Ann became well known for her clothes designs. She had used her imagination.

Lawrence Emmet learned to play the piano from the age of 5 on. He became an accomplished pianist by the time he was seventeen. He played piano solos at high school variety shows, in church and he played background, piano pieces for the local melodrama and he played in piano recitals.

Lawrence began experimenting and using his imagination to compose original melodies. Once he wrote out the melody he added embellished chords and arpeggios. His piano pieces sounded very original and entertaining. He played his original, piano compositions downtown at a restaurant. He then joined a professional band. His piano pieces became well known because many people listened to them.

A record studio in Hollywood, California was a place where Lawrence had an opportunity to have his original compositions recorded on records and video tapes. In time, Lawrence Emmet became a famous piano soloist and composer because he used his imagination.

Scott Henderson enjoyed sketching and drawing pictures while he was growing up in a small town in California. He used his imagination as he sketched different drawings with colored pencils and paints. He drew portraits of peoples' faces. He became very accomplished in portrait drawing. In time, he went to County Fairs to sketch portraits of people who came to the County Fair. He was able to earn money as a portrait artist because he used his creative talent and imagination to sketch portraits of people. New opportunities exist for many people.

NINE
SPINNING WHEELS

Clothes have been woven by hand in ancient times. Earlier civilizations did not have electricity to produce woven cloth. Spinning wheels and frames with methods to produce wool and cotton thread were made out of wood and controlled by hands and feet. It took much longer to produce woolen cloth and cotton fabrics because they were handmade.

Electricity was discovered in the early 1800s by Benjamin Franklin. Thomas Edison produced the first light bulbs. Electricity was transmuted in conducting wires to affect the movement of thimbles and wooden spindles. Electricity has speeded up the production of cloth and various kinds of fabric.

Nylons are made with electric thimbles. They once were produced with wooden, hand and foot thimbles which move up and down.

Harry Wignall created electric thimbles which move quickly up and down to produce nylon thread. Nylon thread is made into hosiery. Nylon stockings have been worn in the 1920s on. Women protect their legs and feet with nylon stockings.

Harry Wignall was the first to create a large manufacturing of nylon stockings in the 1930s in Leister, England. His nylon stockings are still being spun in electrical machines today.

Other hosiery manufacturers are producing nylon stockings in different sizes and colors today.

Spinning wheels are still used in small villages in Europe. Thread is still spun by more primitive cultures where modern manufacturing methods are not available. Thread is dyed different colors after wool or cotton is spun and are spun in wooden frames called looms.

Spun thread is made into cloth and fabric to produce clothes of all types. Woolen sweaters are made by hand in Scotland, Ireland and parts of England. Lace is used to make curtains, doilies, tablecloths and used for rims on clothes and even underwear. The lace is spun on special looms. The lace is handspun to use as decorative designs on clothes, such as collars and sleeves.

The handmade method of spinning wool and cotton should not become a lost art. Older generations should continue to teach younger generations to use spinning wheels.

TEN
WHY SETTLE FOR MORE

Why should we settle for less when we can settle for more? Many people have been taught to think they are not entitled to a more prosperous life. As a result these people tend to go without certain benefits and luxuries because they have less money. They are afraid to spend more especially if they can't afford expensive things.

Life is to be lived to the fullest. A person can learn to prosper and acquire certain worthwhile items and material possessions. It is unrealistic to buy extremely expensive jewelry, clothes, cars, boats and houses especially if a person doesn't have much money. It is important to live within one's economic range. A $10,000 fur coat should not be purchased if a woman is living on a meager, annual salary. An expensive million dollar yacht should not be purchased if a person is living on a small, annual income.

In other words, a person should live within his or her realistic budget in order to pay the monthly bills which must be paid. To overspend a limited income is the way to become broke. Living within one's personal income is the best way to survive financially. It is wise to balance one's bank account every month.

We can spend more money for things we desire if we save enough money for these luxuries. Without sufficient funds we should not write checks which may bounce. We should be sure enough money is in our bank accounts.

Wealthy people have plenty of money to spend. They can afford expensive clothes, jewelry, cars, boats, houses and food. Wealthy people should be aware of how much money they are spending to be sure they don't overspend what they have accumulated.

It is wise to do one's own bookkeeping in order to protect one's own money. If someone else takes care of your bookkeeping you need to hire someone who is trustworthy and honest. If you employ someone who is not trustworthy this person may steal money from your bank accounts.

Barbara Hutton was a wealthy millionaire because she inherited her parents wealth. She employed lawyers and bookkeepers to keep track of her millions of dollars. She trusted her lawyers and bookkeepers to handle her finances. The lawyers and bookkeepers misspent her money. They even robbed her bank accounts. Barbara Hutton was nearly penniless when she died because her millions of dollars were stolen.

A black man was poor when he began a chocolate chip cookie enterprise. He baked delicious cookies and packaged them to sell. He began selling his cookies to people in the street and eventually he distributed his cookies to many grocery stores. People bought his cookies. So, many cookies were bought. In time, he became a millionaire because his chocolate chip cookies were sold around America. He invested his money wisely and remained wealthy. He managed his own finances and he didn't overspend his wealth.

Individuals who start from scratch with little money may become wealthy because they are entrepreneurs. They are willing to risk spending a certain amount to start a new business. They invest their money carefully and conserve their financial gains in order to reinvest so they can earn more money. They don't allow anyone to misuse their wealth.

Donald Trump, an American businessman, invested money into large hotels around different cities. He has accumulated over ten large hotels. Some hotels are in Las Vegas, Nevada. Donald Trump has become a billionaire.

ELEVEN
UNDERSTANDING WHY?

Understanding why certain experiences occur a certain way helps an individual become aware of life. Understanding Cosmic laws of the Universe explains why the Cosmos functions within these laws.

What are some Cosmic laws? The Cosmic laws are universal love, cause and effect, gravitation, polarities (opposites such as positive and negative), electromagnetism, balance and equilibrium, centralization, unity, harmony and interdimensional space. There are other Cosmic laws that exist which humanity may learn about in time.

Understanding how the universe was created is fascinating. The universe is made up of different dimensions. There is the physical universe and the higher etheric universe. Each dimension has a purpose for existing. Scientists recently have stated that there are parallel universes which exist in different dimensions. Scientists are learning to understand why the universe is dimensional.

NASA Space Program sends out cameras to photograph and to film outer space. Photographs and films indicate the surface of the Earth's Moon, Mars, Europa, a moon going around Jupiter, Saturn, Uranus and Pluto. The surfaces of these planets and moon have been photographed and filmed. Scientists have more understanding of our solar system.

Why is it important to understand the universe? Humanity should learn why and how the universe was created. We should learn all we can learn about how the universe operates. It is believed by astronomers and science professors that the universe is like a big bubble within other bubbles which are universes. Inner dimensions exist within each universe.

The nature of matter has been observed and studied. Matter is known to be solid because particles are closer together. Liquids have particles moving around quickly and much farther apart. Liquids are not solid. Gases are condensed steam and liquid which has evaporated. Gases lift up into the atmosphere. Solids remain on the Earth. Liquids change form and shape within their surroundings.

We should learn about solids, liquids and gases in nature. We should learn how and why plants and animals live and exist on Earth. We should learn about the Earth. Why are there many oceans? How did land masses form? When did the Earth come into existence? How is the ecosystem functioning? Why is it important to maintain balance in the Earth's ecosystem? These are some questions to think about and to find intelligent answers about.

We should be inquisitive and learn all we can about God's creation. We will have more understanding about many creations. As we learn more and more, we develop more understanding about life. We should try to maintain cosmic laws in order to develop and to grow spiritually.

The law of centralization affects our universe and our solar system. Cells have a central nucleus with the life plan or blueprint for specific cells which form in creations such as plants, animals and human beings. The Sun is the center of our solar system. We depend on the light and energy of the Sun to survive. Every living creation has a central existence such as a brain, heart and nervous system. We need to understand how Cosmic laws function in our human and spiritual bodies.

TWELVE
FACING CRISES

Many people face crises in their lives. People experience serious accidents in cars, trains, buses and airplanes. Many people experience serious illnesses such as pneumonia, bronchitis, scarlet fever, the plague, measles, mumps and chicken pox. Other people may become homeless because they do not have a regular income. They lost their homes because they could not afford to pay rent or to buy a house. Many people have suffered because of sudden floods, earthquakes, typhoons, cyclones and hurricanes.

How should we face crises? We need to face crises with acceptance, forgiveness and endurance. We need to be prepared for crises and tragedies by developing a positive attitude and strategies to face crises and tragedies.

Emma Wilson was an elementary school teacher. She began teaching when she was twenty-three once she graduated from college. She had been teaching twelve years. She bought a three bedroom home in an attractive neighborhood in Buffalo, New York, where she grew up. Emma was a successful teacher.

Little did Emma realize that she would have a sudden, tragic accident in her car. She was driving carefully one day downtown on her way home from work. While Emma was driving down a side street, which was a shortcut to her residence, suddenly a truck was coming towards her car from the opposite side of the street. The street was dark because the streetlights had not been turned on.

The truck was going 50 miles an hour in a 30 mile an hour zone. As the truck driver in the truck approached Emma's car, he didn't realize how narrow the street was. His truck collided into Emma's car causing her car to crash and turn over several times. Consequently, Emma was badly injured. As soon as the accident was reported by some witnesses to the police station, several policemen drove to the scene of the accident.

Paramedics assisted Emma onto a stretcher and they carried her into an ambulance. The ambulance drivers took Emma to the nearest hospital to the Emergency Ward. She was examined by several doctors on duty. X-rays were taken of her bones and body parts. Emma was in a coma. She was put into the Intensive Care Unit.

Emma was put on a life support system. A breathing tube was put in her mouth. A catheter was placed inside of her urethra. Emma's heart was carefully monitored. Emma remained in a coma. She had been injured severely by the enormous truck. However, she was still alive. For how long no one knew. She was kept in Intensive Care for several months. During this time doctors took care of Emma's fractures and one broken arm and leg. Emma was bruised all over as well.

After two months in Intensive Care, Emma was moved to the regular care unit. She was carefully monitored even then. She hadn't been able to leave her hospital bed for months. She still was in a coma. Nurses, doctors and visitors tried to wake her up. They talked to her and touched her hands, arms and face. Emma didn't respond.

Then, one day several months later, there was a loud booming sound outside. It was so loud that this booming sound jarred many people. People sleeping woke up suddenly because they heard the loud sound. Emma responded to the loud booming sound. She finally woke up.

Emma opened her eyes slowly. She looked around the hospital room. There was a man in the bed across the hospital room. He was watching television. Emma wondered where she was. She couldn't remember what had happened to her.

Emma gradually moved her hands and feet while she was in bed. She finally looked over at the man in the other bed. She wondered why she was in a room with a stranger. She felt weak and she had lost much of her memory. A nurse came into her hospital room. The nurse, Miss Hopkins, noticed that Emma was finally awake.

Miss Hopkins went up to Emma's bed to speak to her. Miss Hopkins said, "Good! You are awake!" Emma stared at this nurse, who she did not know. She finally spoke. "Where am I," Emma asked. Miss Hopkins replied, "You are in the hospital." Emma asked, "Why am I in the hospital?" The nurse answered, "You were in a bad accident several months ago!"

Emma looked concerned. She asked, "Where was the accident?" Miss Hopkins replied, "You were in an accident downtown. A truck driver hit your car." Emma touched her head with her hands. She felt pain in her body. She knew she had been in an accident. Emma appeared very upset. Miss Hopkins said, "Please keep calm. We thought you would never wake up."

Emma laid in her hospital bed wondering why she was in an accident. She couldn't remember what had happened. She moved her legs in bed. She attempted to get up. But, she was unable to get up. She was too weak and she felt helpless. She realized that she was trapped in bed.

Emma felt depressed and worried about her physical condition. She couldn't remember her name or where she lived. She was in a state of confusion. Her future seemed dim. She was facing a serious crisis.

Dr. Tompkins, who was Emma's doctor at the hospital in Buffalo, New York, walked into Emma's hospital room. He stood by Emma's hospital bed and he said, "Hello. I am Dr. Tompkins. How are you feeling?" Emma stared at Dr. Tompkins bleakly. She replied, "I ache all over. I wish I could get out of bed." Dr. Tompkins replied, "You have been in a bad accident. We almost lost you. It will take more time for you to recover. You have been in a coma for two months. I am glad you are finally awake."

SIGNIFICANT MOMENTS

Emma had tears in her eyes because she felt so downhearted. Dr. Tompkins examined Emma carefully. A nurse came into the hospital room to take Emma's pulse and temperature. Emma's pulse was slightly high and her body temperature was 99.5. Dr. Tompkins continued to speak to Emma. He said, "Now that you have come out of your coma we will be able to treat your condition better. You will need physical therapy to regain your physical strength. It will take time for you to walk again. You broke your left leg and your left arm. They will continue to mend in time. Can you remember your name?"

Emma tried to remember her name. She answered Dr. Tompkins's question. "I don't remember my name or where I live." Dr. Tompkins replied, "According to your I.D. which was found during your accident, your name is Emma Wilson. You live on Cypress Street in Buffalo." Emma looked at Dr. Tompkins. Her name and residence didn't sound familiar to her. She responded, "I don't remember this name or address. Will I be able to remember who I am soon?" Dr. Tompkins replied, "It may take some time for you to get your memory back. You had a severe concussion in your brain which shocked your brain cells. You will have to be patient. In time you may be able to function normally again. I will be checking on your condition every day. I will be back again tomorrow morning. You should try to eat some breakfast this morning now that you are awake."

Emma still had tears in her eyes. The nurse was still standing near Emma's hospital bed. She said, "I will have someone bring you some breakfast." Emma stared at the nurse. Dr. Tompkins left the hospital room to continue his rounds around the hospital ward.

Meanwhile, someone brought a tray of breakfast to Emma's bed. A nurse helped Emma sit up in bed so she could eat. The tray of food was placed near Emma. There were scrambled eggs, orange juice, hash browns and toast as well as sliced fruit. Emma looked at the food. The nurse said, "Try to eat your breakfast." Emma had forgotten how to use a fork, spoon and knife. The nurse said, "Here is your breakfast." Emma looked at the food. She didn't pick up the fork, spoon or knife. The nurse realized that Emma needed help to eat. The nurse picked up the fork and put scrambled eggs on the fork. She fed Emma scrambled eggs. She said, "You can pick up your toast to eat." Emma finally picked up a piece of toast. She began eating it. The nurse picked up some orange juice in a glass and encouraged Emma to drink it. Emma swallowed some orange juice. Then the nurse encouraged Emma to pick up the fork to eat some hash browns. She showed Emma how to use her fork. Emma finally learned to use her fork. She continued eating her breakfast.

Emma was given physical therapy treatments every day thereafter to strengthen her body. She gradually regained more body strength and dexterity. Step by step Emma gradually began to remember different experiences in her life. Amnesia was a challenging experience in her life.

Friends and relatives came to the hospital to visit with Emma. They tried to help Emma to recall experiences in her life. Her memory gradually and slowly returned. Friends and relatives encouraged Emma to get well. They knew she had been suffering from a serious, automobile accident.

Emma remained physically handicapped for a long time. She was unable to go back to her residence. She was unable to go back to her teaching position because of her handicaps. She tried to accept and adjust to her situation. She attended group therapy to talk about how she felt about her handicaps and new life. Group therapy helped Emma to relate to others and it gave her an opportunity to express her thoughts and feelings.

THIRTEEN
VOYAGERS

VOYAGERS, written by Ashayana Deane, is information transcribed from the Guardian Alliance regarding Extraterrestrial Visitation, the Extraterrestrial Agenda, Keylontic Morphogenetic Science and the Mechanics of Alien Contact. VOYAGERS is a set of books asking the question: "What do we really know about the nature of reality," stated by Ashayana Deane.

Ashayana Deane has studied, investigated and carefully examined information and findings about other worlds and our origins and the nature of reality itself. She stated, "In our contemporary world we are progressively presented with more and more experiences and occurrences of an extraordinary nature. Over the last 20 years alone it seems as if the extraordinary has taken on a life of its own. People now routinely report extraordinary experiences such as psychic phenomena, out-of-body experiences, hauntings, channeling of disembodied spirits, visitations by angels, sightings of UFOs and abduction by aliens, etc."

Ashayana Deane mentions that ancient Sumerian, Egyptian, Greek and Roman civilizations experienced extraordinary visitations by gods and demons from other worlds. The visitors from elsewhere were feared and worshipped by ancient man.

The foundations of most ancient cultures were built upon a literal acknowledgment of unseen worlds.

Ashayana Deane believes that our scientific communities tend to view the otherworld beliefs of contemporary humans and ancient cultures in symbolic terms, considering them to be representations of psychological archetypes of the times, rather than as valid evidence for human contact with other worlds.

Ashayana Deane believes it is quite possible that ancient records included both symbolic and literal representations of reality. She stated that, "Our contemporary interpretations of ancient records may not fully reflect the actualities those records were intended to describe and our potential interpresentation of ancient events may cause us to misinterpret the extraordinary events of today."

Ashayana Deane claims that "the majority of our ancient races left evidence suggesting that contact from elsewhere served an integral role within the very structure of their sociological organization. From the polytheistic, pantheistic, pagan and monotheistic religions of the ancients through the rich historical tapestries of cultured mythology and up to the religious traditions we hold most dear today, humans have demonstrated awareness of the existence of other inhabited worlds."

Ashayana Deane stated that "the majority of collective humanity has validated within their belief paradigms, the existence of unseen worlds inhabited by intelligent beings that periodically interacted with human culture." She continued by stating, "Within the traditional, New Age and indigenous religious communities of the present day and throughout future times humanity has evolved step by step."

Ashayana Deane stated that, "planets assumed to be uninhabitable could actually support subterranean, surface or etheric civilizations of evolved life forms that are not yet known to exist. All planets and galaxies in the universe can be perceived, located and identified through modern, technological instrumentation. The existence of all possible worlds can be theorized through contemporary mathematic computation."

"The facts are that other worlds, supporting advanced civilizations, may appear unseen from today's scientific perspective because they exist in dimensions (or fields of frequency) unknown to contemporary science. We have accepted the scientific assumption that ancient recorded accounts of other world contacts represent the symbolic folly of a less developed primitive mind and thus we discount the possible implications of those ancient records. Our ancient ancestors were aware of extraterrestrial beings and ancient civilizations. It is possible that ancient civilizations were more advanced in their way of life than we are today. It is erroneous to think our present civilizations are the only advanced cultures on Earth."

Ancient civilizations have come and gone. Advanced civilizations have disappeared such as Sumerians, Egyptians, Romans and Babylonians. Even if they were advanced they made mistakes. They experienced wars, famine and diseases. They lost their power because of corruption.

Extraterrestrial civilizations have lived in high mountains and other remote places. Ashayana Deane suggests "that visiting representatives from otherworld cultures may have directly influenced the evolution of human culture on Earth. Our religious belief systems of today may have their roots in otherworld cultures. Ashayana Deane asked the question, "What if we were put here to evolve, by an Elder Race of interstellar, inter-time or inter-dimensional visitors as the propagation of their genetics?"

The Elder Races were created through a Divine Source. This suggests that our Divine Source had created greater diversity of form than that which is apparent on Earth. God's creations included the E.T.,OD (Other-dimensional) and IT (Inter-time) inhabitants of the Otherworld, as well as human and other life forms on Earth. The possibility of non-terrestrial genetic origin does to negate our intrinsic connection to a Divine Source. We often assume that God is created in the image of man.

Visiting races from Otherworld Homo sapien races and earthly primate forms could easily account for the genetic similarities between certain primate, primitive hominid and Homo sapiens species. We may be progenitors instead of being the descendents of primitive man.

Ashayana Deane described types of UFOs. She said that three-dimensional, mechanical-type UFOs can be placed into the following four categories. The first type belong to covert government operations who will maintain a policy of non-disclosure and denial regarding sightings of their crafts. The second type are those representing interdimensional anomalies from parallel systems that appear as vessels but in actuality represent other phenomena as they appear when interfacing with your system. The third type of UFO is an actual craft from other dimensions that emerge through the Time and Dimensional Portal Systems. The fourth type of UFO is an actual craft belonging to human or extraterrestrial cultures that emerge through the Time Portal System from locations within the third-dimensional universe.

In all these cases the UFO craft appear physically solid; some having material wreckage left behind as validation of their existence. There are other highly intelligent non-human species residing in our universe. Light-formation sightings are not accidental dimensional interface phenomena or natural atmospheric anomalies from interdimensional probes. There exists an enormous variety of sentient, intelligent life.

There are time zones within our universe as well as multiple dimensions of these time zones. "Alien" visitors or extraterrestrials have been visiting the Earth for thousands of years. Types of extraterrestrials are Zeta Reticules, Little Greys, Aethiens, Rhanthias, Zionites, Borendts and more.

The Zionist strain constitutes a master race of beings whose abilities and powers reach far beyond the present moment of your Earth history. This race was created by "splicing together" the best of the human strain with other highly advanced genetic material from other systems. The Zionites were genetic experimentations of the Zeta in conjunction with the Athien. Their strain is unique in its abilities of maneuverability through time. From their points of origin in a dimension of Earth adjacent to your own, and running along a time continuum parallel to that of your present, the Zionites have fanned outward in time within your third dimension and also within other dimensions. There are planets within our universe in which Zionites can be found and there are large groupings of them working with the Aethiens in their own systems. Zionites are part of our heritage on Earth. Zionites are part of our future and our past.

SIGNIFICANT MOMENTS

Earthlings have been abducted by extraterrestrial beings who have come to Earth to contact Earthlings. Greys have captured Earthlings in remote places. Extraterrestrial beings are observing and experimenting with their abductees to find out how human beings function and live.

Women, who have been selected to carry an embryo or fetus, are those who carry some trace of the Silicate Matrix within their latent generic code. Their bodies are able to endure some degree of transmutation. Women, who have the abduction experience of missing fetuses or vanishing pregnancies, fall into another category. These women are not simply "egg donors" but serve as surrogate mothers for another version of the "white" hybrid.

VOYAGERS is an informative book about Visitors and human origins, mysteries, missing evidence, particle transmition and time. Human origins and hybridization, as well as interdimensional communications, twelve tribes and crop circles exist. There are many more stimulating topics.

FOURTEEN
EXTRASENSORY EXPERIENCES

Extrasensory experiences can occur readily. Some individuals are psychic. So, they are able to see visions and experience aberrations. The astral plane is invisible to the physical eyes. The third eye is an invisible eye which is used to visualize the astral plane, an invisible plane which is parallel to the physical plane.

Ellen Scotsdale grew up in a conventional home and she was raised by parents who were Christians. She was taught that Jesus Christ is our savior and only Lord. Ellen was never exposed to metaphysical books and extrasensory experiences while she was growing up. She focused on her five senses known as sight, sound, touch, taste and smell. Ellen looked at the Earth and nature on the physical plane. She used her ears to listen to many sounds such as the chirping of birds, crashing waves in the ocean, vehicle sounds, human voices and musical instruments, etc. Ellen smelled fragrances, odors and observed many nature creations on Earth. Ellen was familiar with touching Earthly and manmade objects. Ellen tasted a variety of foods.

Ellen was not aware of extrasensory experiences until she was 30 years old. Ellen had married at the age of 25. Her husband, Frank, was a conventional person with a Christian, religious background. He did not believe in extrasensory perception or in extraterrestrial beings.

Frank and Ellen lived in a three bedroom house in a town near Santa Barbara, California, called Solvang. Ellen's parents lived in Santa Ynez, which was five miles south of Solvang. When Ellen was 30 years old her mother, Virginia Morris passed away after suffering from heart failure.

Ellen mourned for many months because of her mother's death. She missed her mother because she was very close to her mother while she was living. Ellen was able to talk to her mother about very personal problems and concerns happening in her life.

Ellen continued to think about her mother. She cried frequently because of her grief over her mother's death. One day when Ellen woke up suddenly she saw her mother standing near her bed. Ellen was very surprised and startled to see her mother. Ellen noticed that her mother looked younger and radiant.

Virginia, Ellen's deceased mother, looked at Ellen with a loving expression. Virginia spoke to Ellen. She said, "Ellen, don't be startled. I have come to visit with you. Listen to my thoughts. I am in my spirit body." Ellen decided to respond verbally to her mother's spirit body. She said, "You look younger and happier. What is it like on the spirit plane?"

Virginia spoke gently. She continued. "Heaven is very beautiful and peaceful. I am happy in my new heavenly home. When I passed away I traveled through a bright tunnel to another realm." Ellen was eager to hear more from her deceased mother. She asked her mother, "Have you seen Jesus Christ?" Virginia responded, "Jesus Christ was near me when I passed from Earth. Jesus guided me to the next realm. I was greeted by loved ones on the other side."

Ellen was amazed that her deceased mother had appeared before her that morning. Virginia suddenly disappeared as quickly as she had appeared. She had communicated with her daughter. Ellen felt better now that her mother had appeared before her that morning. Ellen stopped grieving for her mother. She went on with her life accepting that her mother was happy and well adjusted in Heaven.

Ellen Scotsdale had an extrasensory experience. She saw her deceased mother with her third eye or inner eye. This unusual experience helped Ellen realize that life continues on the next realm known as Heaven. Ellen was no longer afraid to die. She knew life was eternal.

FIFTEEN
NEW AGE MUSIC

New Age music is very etheric. Musical instruments have a special effect such as certain flutes, guitars, clavichords and pianos. Ancient instruments made in China and India have a distant, unusual sound.

Indian chants can be sung with unusual effects to create distant sounds. Spiritual tones can be sounded on harps, horns, violins, guitars and Asian string instruments.

New Age music arouses a sense of upliftment and spiritual awareness. Celestial music elates many listeners. More and more worthwhile music has been composed. This New Age music has been recorded on records, DVDs and videos. Nature sounds such as ocean waves and wind is also recorded.

Certain music is presented on Channel 936 on cable television sponsored by Charter. Many unusual melodies and spiritual verses are being presented. This background music is relaxing to listen to. New Age music can help bring peace and joy to many listeners.

SIXTEEN
CELESTIAL AWARENESS

Celestial realms exist in our Cosmic plan. Interdimensional space exists. Heavenly realms are visible and invisible spheres. Many celestial spheres move within other spheres.

Celestial rhythm and cycles exist. A Cosmic Breath occurs at cyclic intervals. Suns, planets and planetoids move in given directions in a cyclic pattern in rhythm with each other. Suns effect the movement of planets and planetoids.

Each solar system is like a cell in the body of the universe. The laws of gravitation and electromagnetism, polar opposites, law of motion and rhythm promote balance and equilibrium in each solar system. Each constellation is made up of many solar systems and stars.

Celestial awareness helps us expand our awareness of God's Cosmic creations. Suns are born and eventually they die. A burst of celestial energy causes a star to be created. A black hole sucks a dissolving star in, which is disintegrating in space. Many other stars, planets and planetoids near a dying star may be sucked into a big black hole, while a star is disintegrating.

Our planet Earth is effected by Manvantaras which last 432,000 years each. Our planet is approximately 4 1/2 billion years old. With divine protection our planet may exist for millions of years. Human beings have an opportunity to grow and evolve in different root races.

Celestial light, unity, love and wisdom operate in the celestial cosmos. God's plan exists and promotes the will for cosmic laws to operate effectively in the cosmos. The light of God never fails. Human errors are what cause humanity to believe certain falsehoods about the universe.

Celestial creations are controlled by cause and effect happenings. Each celestial creation effects all creations to some degree. Flame of fohat blaze within galaxies and nebula. Purple, gold, green, blue, pink and white can be seen emanating in the universe.

Our universe is one among many universes. Each universe moves in a spiral motion and as cosmic bubbles in celestial space. Suns in celestial galaxies radiate light and heat. The Milky Way is a large galaxy in our universe. Millions of planets revolve around many suns which are luminous stars. Each universe functions within a celestial sphere within the Divine Creator's Cosmic Blueprint. Each universe revolves in its own celestial orbit in space. Each universe has a cyclic pattern of evolution. Evolution gives life forms in the celestial plan an opportunity to grow and expand. New creations are being created constantly in the universes. New life forms begin with their own blueprint. The law of centralization exists to promote unity, harmony and to create the nucleus within suns and solar systems. Every life form has a center which sustains each life form. The light and blueprint of the Divine Creator exists in each center.

The celestial cosmos has existed for billions and billions of light years. New suns and planets continue to come into existence so that new life forms may be created. Celestial awareness helps us become awakened about our Universe.

SEVENTEEN
FACTS ABOUT ZOOS

Zoos have been established around the world. Zoos have existed for hundreds of years. Wild animals have been captured to put in zoos. A variety of animals such as monkeys, apes, lions, tigers, elephants, giraffes, zebras, gazelles, goats, tropical birds, crocodiles, snakes, turtles, alligators and many more creatures exist in zoos.

Lighting is important at zoos especially at night. Zoo caretakers look after the wild animals on a daily basis. Different scrubs and trees, as well as grass, are planted at zoo grounds to add to a natural environment. Wild animals respond better if they dwell in a more natural setting. Each wild animal needs certain types of food.

Lions, tigers, panthers and bears are carnivorous. They eat raw meat with their canine teeth. Wolves and coyotes are also carnivorous. So, they also eat raw meat. Zoo caretakers put meat in each cage several times a day. Fresh water must be provided several times a day. Wild animals who are not meat eaters are elephants, giraffes, monkeys, apes, zebras, gazelles, deer, goats and sheep. Turtles do not eat meat either. Some snakes may not eat meat. Other snakes are carnivorous. They eat other snakes, rodents, eggs and insects.

SIGNIFICANT MOMENTS

Most birds in a zoo live in large aviaries. Birds are fed seeds, small scraps of fruit and vegetables. They need space to walk around. Flamingos dwell near zoo ponds in flocks. Other birds are peacocks with beautiful plumes. There are parrots and doves. Birds are kept in cages. Bird cages must be cleaned out frequently. Bird dew must be rinsed away from every cage.

The largest zoos in the world are at San Diego, Los Angeles, San Francisco, New York in the U.S.A and in London in England. Zookeepers work at all of these zoos plus many smaller zoos. It is fun to go to the zoo to observe wild animals to observe how they behave and eat.

EIGHTEEN
PLAYING A HARP

Harps are stringed instruments created many hundreds of years ago. Harps have an unusual shape. The strings are put in parallel directions and fastened to wood framing. Harps are played at weddings, funerals and used as important musical instruments in orchestras. Harps are artistic looking musical instruments.

Harps are played in classical concerts at Carnegie Hall, Schubert's Theater, Albert's Hall in London and at the Philadelphia Orchestra in Philadelphia. Harps have many strings which can be seen readily. Shorter strings have a much higher pitch. Longer strings have a lower tone.

A harp player moves his or her fingers up and down on harp strings stroking and plucking the many strings rhythmically. Harps are still well known and they are played by skilled harpists.

NINETEEN
WHITE CLIFFS

W hite cliffs located near the ocean along the coasts of California and in England are very scenic. The White Cliffs of Dover in Dover, England are very well known.

A song entitled WHITE CLIFFS OF DOVER was written about the famous White Cliffs in Dover along the coast. Thousands of seabirds make their nests in nooks and crannies on ledges on the White Cliffs. The scenic, panoramic view of the White Cliffs of Dover can be seen for miles away.

The White Cliffs of Dover are near London, England. Kate Smith, a well known vocal soloist, sang WHITE CLIFFS OF DOVER on the stage and even on television. Many people have traveled to the coast of Dover to see the glistening, white cliffs.

White cliffs can be seen along the coast of Shell Beach, California. These white cliffs are near a restaurant overlooking a marvelous view of the white cliffs. Many seabirds fly back and forth to their nests in the ledges of the white cliffs. These white cliffs have been along Shell Beach coast for thousands of years.

White cliffs exist in other places in the world along sea coasts. Most white cliffs are very scenic because the white, gleaming light on the cliffs stands out for many miles. Tourists generally travel to seacoasts to enjoy cool breezes, scenic views of the ocean and to witness white foam on ocean waves as well as coastal cliffs.

TWENTY
RARE COMMODITIES

Rare commodities are seldom available because they are scarce and difficult to find. Rare jewels are not available in most jewelry shops. Rare specimens of gems are not found in most gem shops.

Clothes designed and worn hundreds of years ago are out of fashion and style today. Men's suits and high neck blouses and dresses are no longer produced in clothing factories. It is rare to come across clothes worn even fifty years ago. Clothing fashions continue to change from generation to generation.

Old Model T Fords are out of style. Many new models of cars are produced today. Cars which were produced from 1925 on are no longer available. Some old models of cars are displayed in museums and special car shows. These old models are rare commodities because few old car models are in existence today.

Rare commodities such as old cars, old fashion clothes, rare jewels and gems are very valuable today because they are very rare.

Original paintings which were painted centuries ago are considered to be rare and very valuable. Sculptures which were created in ancient times are very rare and worth a lot of money today. Original artifacts created long ago are very valuable and rare.

Ancient vases, porcelain bowls, plates and cups with saucers have been put in museums and certain art galleries. These ancient art creations are rare commodities and are very valuable today.

TWENTY-ONE
MIDDLE EAST SOLUTIONS

The Middle East has been a big issue in the news since September 11, 2001 when the World Trade Center was bombed and destroyed. Three thousand or more innocent people were killed during this attack. It was a terrorist from Egypt who affiliated with the Al Qaida Movement who attacked the World Trade Center in New York City in the U.S.A.

Yet, Iraq and Afghanistan became targets regarding the attack on the World Trade Center. Saddam Hussein was accused of attacking America. He had not cooperated with the United Nations regarding the distribution of oil and because of the Kuwait issue in the Middle East. Many oil derricks were burned up so that a lot of oil was wasted. As a result the Bush Administration went to war in 2003 against Iraq.

Trillions of American dollars have been spent for this war in Iraq. Baghdad, in Iraq, was severely attacked. Many palaces and government buildings were bombed and destroyed. Military installations and warfare weapons in Iraq were destroyed. Three years later Saddam Hussein was captured. He was convicted at an Iraqi court for many crimes. In time he was executed in Iraq for his crimes.

George Bush Jr. talked about establishing democratic governments in Iraq and Afghanistan. Over 9 trillion dollars of American tax money and reserves have been spent because of American military and warfare weapons to Iraq and Afghanistan to fight.

The people in Iraq and Afghanistan are lacking food, water and medical supplies. Many Iraqis and Afghans have been killed because of this war. The Iraqis wish that Americans would leave Iraq. They have been voting in free elections. However, Iraqi and Afghan women are not free. They are escorted everywhere by husbands, fathers and brothers when they go outside their homes. Women have no say so. Men make most of the decisions still in Iraq and Afghanistan.

There are solutions to the Middle East problems. Middle Eastern men should be schooled to change their attitudes and beliefs about dominating women. Leaders of the Al Qaida should be caught. Once influential leaders have been captured and imprisoned it will be easier to capture many members of the Al Qaida in order to stop and to prevent them from attacking Americans and Middle Eastern people who want freedom and independence.

Middle Eastern countries need to be educated about the value of democracy and to learn to make better choices. Political leaders of America should find ways to stop the wars in Iraq and Afghanistan as soon as possible. The problem presently is that the Al Qaeda have been spreading around the Middle East and other countries such as The Philippines, South America and parts of Indonesia, etc.

How can the Al Qaeda Movement be stamped out? Many people have been converted to the beliefs and indoctrination of the Al Qaeda Movement. These people need to be exposed to a democratic approach of life. When they have had an opportunity to find out how democracy works for the good of all, then these people will be able to realize the value of democracy and how they can become independent and to be free. They can band together to promote democratic beliefs and actions.

TWENTY-TWO
DIFFERENT BANDS

Bands have formed at least one hundred years ago. Well known bands were formed by band leaders. The Harry James Band started in the 1920s. The John Phillips Souza Band formed in the early 1900s. The Glen Miller Band formed in the 1930s. The Benny Goodman Band formed in the 1940s. The Lawrence Welk's Band became well known in the 1950s. Louis Armstrong's band was formed in the 1950s.

Each band has a unique style of music. Each band dresses in unique costumes. Each band leader has become an accomplished musician. Harry James played a horn. John Phillip Souza played several musical instruments. Glen Miller played the trumpet and saxophone. Benny Goodman played the clarinet. Lawrence Welk played the accordion.

Band arrangements distinguish one band from another. Harry James had sophisticated band arrangements. John Phillip Souza focused on marching band arrangements. Glen Miller developed a new style by focusing on certain horn arrangements. Benny Goodman focused on clarinet solos in his band. Louis Armstrong developed unique jazz band arrangements. Lawrence Welk developed champagne music. He played his accordion as a solo instrument. His band played popular band pieces.

Bands perform in parades at festivals and holiday celebrations. Bands add to special celebrations. Band players learn to march in parades. They wear band uniforms which are colorful and attractive.

Generally, children who learn to play band instruments such as the clarinet, trumpet, saxophone, flute, drums and xylophone, etc, join the school band. They learn to play in rhythm as each musical instrument is played. Band music is used. School bands continue to perform in parades and at festivals and concerts.

TWENTY-THREE
ICECREAM TREATS

Icecream has become a popular treat. There are over 50 flavors of icecream. Well known icecream flavors are strawberry, vanilla, chocolate, mint, orange, pineapple, coconut, pistachio, maple, blueberry, blackberry, boysenberry and more.

Icecream can be served in different ways. Icecream can be served in cones, in scoops in dishes and in sundaes. Icecream is served inside cake. Icecream milkshakes are prepared with a variety of flavors.

Icecream is prepared with iced milk and different flavors and some sugar. Icecream is served as dessert for lunch and dinner. Icecream is served at parties, receptions, wedding receptions, celebrations, at festivals, etc.

A banana-split sundae is made with chocolate, strawberry and vanilla icecream scoops, sliced banana and chocolate sauce. The icecream scoops are spread out in an oval dish. Banana slices are spread around the icecream. The chocolate sauce is spread over the icecream scoops and bananas. Whipped cream is spread over the banana split sundae. A cherry is placed on the top on the whipped cream.

Icecream is a popular treat. It was created hundreds of years ago once refrigeration was created. Refrigeration is necessary so iced milk can harden to produce icecream.

Many people enjoy eating icecream at home, restaurants, at parties, festivals, extravaganzas, receptions and at church banquets, etc. Icecream will continue to be eaten by many people.

TWENTY-FOUR
SERVERS ARE PEOPLE

Servers who work in restaurants, cafes and fast service establishments have feelings and they react to the behaviour of customers. Servers usually try to maintain a courteous disposition when they are waiting on customers.

Some customers are impatient, discourteous and critical to servers. They want their food orders right away. Some customers are very critical about food prepared by cooks and chefs in restaurants. Too much seasoning may be used. Or, the food is overcooked or undercooked. Sometimes the wrong order is brought to a customer.

Servers try to please their customers. They want to receive tips from their customers. Servers appreciate customers who are courteous and who appreciate their service. Servers feel better when customers are pleasant to them.

Silvia Holmes was a server at a large restaurant in Houston, Texas called The Enchanters. She had been working at this restaurant for eight years. She was an experienced waitress. Silvia tried to be courteous and efficient as a server. She had a reputation of being an excellent server. She worked five days a week on different shifts. On Monday, Tuesday and Wednesday she worked from 7 a.m. to 3p.m. On Thursday and Friday she worked from 2 p.m. until 10 p.m.

Silvia was capable of serving many tables in a short period of time. She wrote down each order carefully and placed the orders on a clip holder near the cooks' area. The cooks would read each order before preparing each order. Silvia picked up each order near the cook's station. She took each order to the correct table and placed the food on the table before each customer.

Silvia encountered customers who were impatient and critical. She tried to be diplomatic and courteous to each customer no matter how they acted. If customers complained about the food she took the food back to the cooks to prepare again. If customers were in a hurry to receive their food she told the cooks to hurry with their orders.

Silvia knew many customers who came to eat at The Enchanters restaurant regularly. She greeted them warmly. She often had casual conversations with them. She usually received good tips from her regular customers.

Silvia made an effort to please all her customers. One day six new customers came into The Enchanters for dinner on a Friday night. The restaurant was filled with many customers. The six newcomers had to wait 45 minutes to be seated at a table. By then they were very hungry and restless. Silvia was very busy serving other customers. After 15 minutes she finally came to the six newcomers' table. She brought menus to their table.

Silvia was tired. She tried to appear pleasant despite how she felt. She asked these six customers if they wanted something to drink. Albert, a 45year old man, ordered root beer. Sharon, a 42 year old woman, ordered ice tea. Scott, who was 18 years old, ordered hot chocolate. Mary, who was 15, ordered Diet Sprite. Joe, who was 13, ordered a coke. Felicia, who was 10, ordered milk.

Silvia wrote down the 6 drinks and walked away to prepare each drink. She was gone for 5 minutes. She brought back the 6 drinks to their table and placed them on their table before each customer. Silvia asked each of them what they wanted to order. Albert ordered a steak dinner with mashed potatoes, string beans and clam chowder. Sharon ordered fried chicken with French Fries and cole slaw. She also ordered clam chowder. Scott ordered prime ribs with a baked potato and mixed, steamed vegetables, plus vegetable soup. Mary, Joe and Felicia ordered hamburgers with French fries and cole slaw. They had clam chowder.

Silvia wrote down the 6 orders and took the orders back to the kitchen and placed the 6 orders on a clip holder. She poured the 6 bowls of soup and brought the soup to the 6 customers' table. She placed the soup before each customer. The 6 customers began eating their soup. Silvia walked away from the table to serve other customers.

While Silvia was busy with other customers, the 6 new customers continued to eat their soup. Albert noticed a fly in his clam chowder after he had sipped several spoons of soup. He complained to Sharon, who was sitting next to him. Sharon told him to tell Silvia, their server about the fly. Albert tried to flag her down. Silvia was so busy. So, she didn't notice Albert. He became frustrated and annoyed because Silvia didn't notice him. Finally he stood up and whistled loudly to get her attention.

Silvia finally noticed Albert whistling to get her attention. She came over to his table. Albert said, "There is a fly in my soup!" Silvia said, "I am sorry. I will get you another bowl of clam chowder." Albert replied, "I hope flies are not in the large container of soup!" Silvia replied, "We keep a lid on the soup container. We try to keep flies away from all the food."

Silvia took Albert's clam chowder away and placed it in a large, dirty dish container. She brought back another clean bowl of clam chowder and placed the soup before Albert. Albert stared at the soup and he examined it carefully. There were no flies in this bowl of soup. He began eating his soup. Meanwhile, Silvia went back to the kitchen to pick up the 6 orders of food. She brought the 6 orders on a large tray.

Silvia placed each order before each customer. She smiled and said, "Enjoy your food." Do you need anything else?" Sharon replied, "We need more bread and butter." Silvia responded, "I will bring more bread and butter." Silvia left the table to get the bread and butter. She brought back more bread and butter. She poured more water in each glass. Silvia did her best to please these customers.

Albert, Sharon, Scott, Mary, Joe and Felicia began eating their dinners. Sharon noticed that her fried chicken was reddish and raw in the center of a breast. She stopped eating her fried chicken. She tried to get Silvia's attention. Silvia was busy serving other customers. She was so busy she didn't notice Sharon. Albert stood up and whistled loudly. Silvia finally noticed Albert. She came over to his table. Sharon complained about her chicken being raw. Silvia apologized about the raw chicken. Silvia took the chicken back to the kitchen. She told the cook to cook the chicken better until it was thoroughly cooked.

Then Silvia brought the fried chicken back to Sharon. Sharon tasted the chicken. It was properly cooked. She continued to eat her chicken dinner. Silvia asked the 6 customers if they wanted some dessert. Albert and Sharon ordered apple pie a la mode. Scott had a strawberry milkshake. Mary Joe and Felicia had custard with whipped cream.

After dinner the 6 new customers were full and satisfied. Silvia came over and said, "I hope you enjoyed your dinners. Please come back again. "She put the dinner bill on the table near Albert. She asked, "Would you like anything else?" Albert and Sharon requested some hot coffee to top off their dinner.

Albert went to pay the bill of $105 at the cashier counter. He came back to the table. He left a $10 tip for Silvia. Then the 6 customers left the restaurant. Silvia went on serving other customers. She was sorry that the newcomers had experienced a fly in the soup and tasted raw chicken. She hoped this wouldn't happen again. She was very tired by 9 p.m. She still had another hour to work. She went on working until 10 p.m. She received more tips from her customers.

TWENTY-FIVE
OUR ECONOMY TODAY

The American economy within the last number of years of 2005 to 2009 has been floundering because of the high cost of the Middle Eastern war. Trillions of dollars have been spent on the Middle Eastern wars. As a result money needed for healthcare, education and public services is not available.

Many people are out of work. These people do not have enough money to pay their bills. They are becoming homeless and more dependent on the general public for food and even shelter. Free meals are served daily at churches and community centers.

If far less money was spent on wars the money could be used to pay for needy people who are in need of food and shelter. People may receive more jobs when there is more money to establish jobs.

When the Wall Street Stock Market fails stocks go down so low that stockholders lose a lot of money. More money must be used to restore businesses such as car sales establishments, banks and other businesses. Without enough money the economy suffers. Large businesses need to continue to produce money making projects and products.

Depressions are caused by an economy that is not thriving sufficiently to prosper by buying and selling money products and resources. When 20% or more of the population are out of work this causes the economy to drop.

Many people suffer when there are no jobs and economic resources to benefit their needs. A poor economy causes a slump in opportunities and benefits. Merchandise is not sold.

The American dollar has gone down considerably in value. The American dollar is only worth about 50 cents today. Inflation is the cause of the American dollar to lose a lot of value. The American dollar should go up in value and worth in order to improve the American economy.

If more jobs and economic opportunities become available the economy will be able to improve again. Perhaps a new currency system could be established where the value of money is protected. A world currency may be the answer and solution where inflation is avoided.

Big businessmen and women who have money should create jobs for people in need of work. If more and more people are working to earn a living to pay their bills this will help solve the economic crisis. The economy can be balanced if the government money is distributed wisely to meet the needs of the masses of people.

TWENTY-SIX
INTRIGUING BAHAMA ISLANDS

T he Bahama Islands are located in the Atlantic Ocean off the coast of Florida and below Florida. The Bahamas are a chain of 700 islands in the North Atlantic Ocean. This chain of islands is called an archipelago. Scattered near the larger islands are more than 2,000 rocky islets and cays.

The Bahama Islands are unique. The country has a bold seafaring history with the influence of pirates. The Bahamians are proud of what they have achieved and look forward to the future. The people speak English. Bahamians accept U.S. and Canadian currency as well as Bahamian dollars and cents.

You can see the same television shows, listen to the same music and talk about the same basketball stars. Bahamian motorists use the left side of the road just like drivers in Great Britain.

The closest U.S. city is Palm Beach, Florida which is approximately 50 miles to the west of Bimini Island in the Bahamas. Other Bahama Islands are hundreds of miles away from Palm Beach. Cuba lies 60 miles to the south. The total land area of the Bahamas is 5,382 square miles with more than 2,000 islands spread over 103,000 square miles of blue water. Some 274,000 Bahamians live on twenty-three islands, with more than half in Nassau, on New Providence Island. Some of the islands are uninhabited.

Most of the Bahamian islands are low and flat, with wide sandy beaches. Some beaches are dotted with intricate shells and pieces of driftwood, while others are as smooth and clean as your living room carpet.

Mount Alvernia, the highest point in the Bahamas, has forests 206 feet above Cat Island. The largest island is Andros. The smallest island is Long Cay. The most populated city is Nassau.

The least populated major island is Rum Cay. There are no fresh water rivers in the Bahamas Islands. The climate is semitropical. The average rainfall during the rainy season is 44 inches. The average rainfall during the dry season is 2 inches. The average summer temperature is 80F. Average winter temperature is 70F. Bahama reefs are at 5 percent of the Earth's reef mass. 60,000 West Indian flamingos dwell on Great Inagua Island, which is one of the Bahama Islands.

It took 104 million years to create the Bahama Islands which are made of coral limestone. Coral was deposited on these banks over millions of years. The sea level has changed many times over the centuries.

Blue holes exist with eerie blue light that filters through the deep water inside them. These holes are often circular with straight sides. "Bailing holes" are formed off many of the islands where freshwater bubbles up from the sea floor. Coral reefs are found on the northern rim of most Bahama Islands. These reefs are made from the skeletons of billions of tiny sea creatures called coral polyps. Over the many centuries the dead polyps pile up to form reefs. Living polyps have brilliant green, orange, red and other bright colors. They are found in warm ocean waters where the currents bring them food.

Polyps need sunlight. So, they grow only in shallow water. A thin coating of topsoil and humus covers the islands rock base. Humus is similar to garden compost---decaying plant matter that helps make soil fertile. Most land in the Bahamas has only a few inches of soil.

Swamps, lakes and ponds dot the surface of many islands, but there are no permanent rivers or streams here. The rainwater seeps through cracks in the rock to large underground reservoirs. This fresh water usually forms a bubble on top of a saltwater pool. A layer of brackish, somewhat salty water lies between the salt water and the fresh water. The brackish water is drinkable, but it leaves a salty aftertaste. On islands like Eleuthera and Little Exuma, the bubbles of fresh water are only a few feet deep.

The Bahamas are often called "the Isles of June" because of their pleasant weather. Even during the rainy season it feels like summer. However, hurricanes known as fierce, tropical storms, may occur between August and November. With winds up to 150 miles per hour, they do a lot of damage. When a hurricane is threatening, everyone flees inland. They try to get away from the high waves that pour over seawalls and docks. Often the raging waters pick up large ships and dump them in the interior of an island. The violent winds peel off roofs, crush buildings, rip down power lines and generally cause great devastation.

The generally pleasant climate owes a lot to the Gulf Stream. This warm ocean current flows around the tip of Florida and continues up the eastern coast off the United States and across to Ireland. The Gulf Stream travels as far north as Canada and then turns east to flow across the Atlantic. There it warms the west coast of Europe, generally keeping that continent's harbors ice-free in the winter.

The Abacos are a chain of islands stretching from Walker's Cay in the north to Hole-in-the-Wall in the south and covering an area of 650 square miles. Apparently 10,000 people live in the quiet villages of the Abacos. Their protected waters and isolated coves make them a fine place for deepwater sailing. Hope Town, on the east coast of Great Abaco, is a popular layover. The town is noted for its candy cane-striped lighthouse. The lighthouse is a short stroll from the harbor. Island residents used to earn a living by salvaging material from wrecked ships.

One hundred circular steps lead to the top of the lighthouse and most visitors agree that the view of the picturesque harbor is worth the climb. From the catwalk you can see the village below.

Andros is a collection of four islands separated by narrow tidal channels. Andros covers an area of 2,300 square miles.

The major towns stand along the northeastern coast while the southern areas are most remote and secluded. The inland lakes, swarming with fish, make Andros a paradise for fishing fans. A 140 mile reef lies along the east side of Andros Island. Scuba divers from all over the world flock here to explore the shallow reef and its surroundings. Close to shore, the seafloor plunges 6,000 feet into an underwater valley called The Tongue of the Ocean.

Bimini is a small chain of islands consisting of North Bimini, South Bimini, Cat Cay and Gun Cay. The Gulf Stream, which sweeps along the western shore, brings marlin, sailfish, blue fin, tuna, wahoo and many other big-game species.

North Bimini is more crowded than the other islands. The streets are so narrow that cars must pull over to let other cars pass and the houses nearly touch. On a clear night, the glow of the city lights of Miami, Florida can be seen from North Bimini.

Eleuthera, the first Bahamian island to be settled, has a population of about 10,000. A band of English families were shipwrecked on the northern end of Eleuthera and they settled there. A rougher group of pirates hung out at Spanish Wells. They set up camps there, seeking freshwater and a safe place to store their stolen treasure. Today most of the people in the village make their living by fishing for "lobster", another name for Bahamian crawfish.

Just off Eleuthera is Harbour Island, famous for its pink sand beaches and clear turquoise waters. They make it "the prettiest island" in the Bahamas. The Exumas, which have 365 cays with magnificent beaches and harbors is an exciting place to go. The cays extend over 130 square miles. The two main islands of Great and Little Exuma are connected by a bridge across Ferry Channel. Some cays consist of uninhabited sand dunes and rocks sprinkled with salt ponds. Some have cliffs that plunge into the surf. Some are covered with dense pine forests. The total population of the Exumas is about 3,500.

Grand Bahama Island covers an area of 530 square miles and is home to 41,000 people. This island is barely 60 feet above sea level. Golf courses, tennis courts, modern hotels and casinos have been built here in the 1960s in the Freeport Lucaya area. The oldest settlement is on the Grand Bahama, West End.

Grand Bahama has the island's largest deepwater harbor, making it easier for freighters to dock. Cement plants, oil refineries and other industries have sprung up next to this harbor. Freeport-Lucaya was founded by Wallace Groves in 1955. Freeport Harbor is the world's largest privately owned harbor. It has a "Garden of the Grooves" which is a 12 acre Garden of Eden with more than 5,000 varieties of shrubs, trees and flowers. There is an International Bazaar, a collection of restaurants and shops designed by a famous Hollywood special-effects artist. With about 80 percent of the population, Nassau and Freeport-Lucaya are the major cultural, political and economic centers of the Bahamas.

Inagua is made up of Great Inagua and Little Inagua, the hottest and driest of the islands. With wide stretches of sand and salt flats, the area has a desert climate. Half of Great Inagua near Lake Rosa is a protected park, a sanctuary and breeding territory for more than 60,000 West Indian flamingos which is the national bird of the Bahamas.

Long Island is 80 miles long and only 4 miles wide. Along the shore, many limestone caves are hidden beneath the sea and several shipwrecks lie in the nearby shallows. This island is noted for its white beaches. Long Island's tough grass once made sheep raising a profitable business. Today a few semi-wild sheep and goats can still be seen wandering about the low hills and dunes. Long Island has a population of approximately 3,400 people who live mostly at Deadmans Cay.

Nassau, the capital of the Bahamas, is located on New Providence Island. About 171,540 people or 60 percent of the country's population, live in this city. Nassau's nightlife sparkles with upscale restaurants, glitzy bars, active dance halls and casinos lit up with lights at Cable Beach and on Paradise Island.

The House of Parliament and the Supreme Court are located here in the governmental and historical center of the Bahamas. The Coral World's undersea laboratory is a place to see stingrays and sharks up close. You can also mail a postcard there in the world's only undersea mailbox.

San Salvador was originally named Guanahoni by Lucayan Indians, its first inhabitants. The island was named San Salvador meaning "Holy Savior" by Christopher Columbus when he discovered this land in 1492. Four monuments include a white cross facing the ocean and mark sites where it is believed the explorer first landed. An underwater plaque marks the spot where his ship anchored.

San Salvador, known as Watling Island, consists of 63 square miles of sand dunes and rocky ridges with the 10 mile long Great Lake in the center. Many of the island's population of some 465 fishermen and their families live in Cockburn Town, on the west coast. On the east coast, the New World Museum houses many Lucayan relics.

Christopher Columbus was the first to visit the area. He wrote at great length in his journal about the island's beauty.

Bahamians love their colorful flowers. Some flowers grow in the wild and some grow in formal English gardens. The islands' tropical flowers include hibiscus, bougainvillea, orchid and oleander. Plants grow year round because of the moderate climate.

Vegetation is heavier on the northwestern islands because they receive up to three times as much rain as islands in the south. Large forests of Caribbean pine exist on Grand Bahama, Abaco, Andros and on New Providence. Grasses, bushes and beautiful orchids grow in the forests where the sun beams through the treetops. On Paradise Island, leafy casuarinas trees form arches over the roads.

The timber business is an important industry on the islands. The lumber was used for boat building, furniture and homes. Today pine plantations stretch in long, ramrod-straight rows on many of the islands. While this ensures a crop for the long-term future, the variety of the natural forests is gone. There are still a few natural forests on the wetter islands of Grand Bahama and Abaco, where evergreen trees reach 30 feet high. A hiker needs a machete or sharp knife to chop through the thick undergrowth.

Farmers often chop down trees to make room for fields. Sometimes they burn off the plant ground cover, leaving a nutrient rich ash that fertilizes their crops. The taller trees are usually left standing for shade. If not constantly cut back or burned off, the brush would crowd out the crops.

Red mangrove, which looks like a bush, is actually a tree with stilt like roots that allow it to grow in shallow swamps. Black mangrove is a taller tree that grows in deeper water. Towering palm trees and shorter palms called palmettos grow almost everywhere on the islands. The thatch-top palm and the cabbage palmetto are found on low-lying land where there is lots of fresh water. The silver-top palm prefers even wetter conditions, growing well on Andros with its abundant rainfall.

Fragrant frangipani bushes grow wherever their hardy roots find a bit of soil. Sea grapes, vines and coco plum bushes are plentiful along the coasts. Their wiry branches and tough leaves stick out of the dunes and their roots help stabilize the shifting sands.

Numerous types of corals make up the reef with wispy sea fans and straw-colored sea feathers. Tube coral look like an explosion of small cylinders growing from a central point. Bush coral has many branches and stems that poke into the moving water like a bush on dry land. Long and heavy Elkhorn coral gets its name because it looks like the antlers on an elk. Other varieties of coral include green cactus, stag horn, scroll, blushing star, brain and golfball coral.

There are 650 varieties of shells. There are sixteen kinds of Wentlettrap Abaco and the waters of Exuma Sound are great places to look for shells.

TWENTY-SEVEN
GREAT BRITAIN YESTERDAY AND TODAY

The earliest monuments of the British Isles are the standing stones erected from about 3000 B.C. Britain was a distant outpost of the Roman Empire, and for over 500 years suffered repeated invasions. From the 16th Century on Great Britain began to expand. Britain created a massive empire on five continents.

The United Kingdom of Great Britain is made up of the countries of England, Scotland, Northern Ireland and Wales, which lies 20 miles north of France. The word "British" refers to the people of the whole United Kingdom including Northern Ireland.

The United Kingdom is one of the world's most industrialized nations. It is a land of great natural beauty from the craggy seacoasts of Northern Ireland and the highlands of Scotland to the soft, green rolling hills of England and Wales. The country has many Stone Age monuments, Roman ruins and medieval castles and cathedrals. The country has many links with other nations and the families of a significant minority of British people come from overseas.

The United Kingdom is a constitutional monarchy which means that the head of the state is the queen, Elizabeth II. This role is ceremonial and the queen has no real political power. The government is led by the prime minister, who is the leader of the political party with the most members of Parliament.

The Union flag popularly known as the Union Jack, symbolizes the administrative union of the countries of the United Kingdom. It is made up of the individual flags of three of its four countries.

The British currency (money) has gone through many changes over the centuries. The current decimal system was introduced in 1971 with 100 "new pence" to the pound. There are coins for 1p, 5p, 10p, 20p, 50p, one pound and two pounds. There are also paper bills for 5, 10, 20, 50 and 100 pounds. In Scotland and WALES coins are minted that bear the respective national symbols of those countries, and these are accepted throughout the UK. Most bills are printed by the Bank of England, but separate bills are issued by several Scottish banks. The Channel Islands, which are located near the north coast of France, also issue their own currency.

Recently there has been a major political debate in the United Kingdom as to whether the country should join the new European currency, the euro. Great Britain plans to use euros soon.

In terms of area the UK is a small country; but it is densely populated with a total of about 59.5 million people. It has roughly the same population as France; but half the land area. England is the most densely populated country in the United Kingdom, with more than 1,000 people per square mile. Scotland has huge areas that are very thinly populated and the average density is only 170 people per square mile.

Ethnic minorities make up about three million of the UK population. 33 percent are of Indian or Bangladeshi origin; 17 percent from the Caribbean Islands and 16 percent from Pakistan. Other significant ethnic minority groups come from China, African and Asian countries.

The UK has a remarkable variety of languages. The official language is English. Welsh is taught in schools in Wales. Many people speak English and Welsh and official documents and road signs are in both English and Welsh. People of the Scottish Highlands and Islands still use many words of Gaelic (a language related to Irish). On the Isle of Man, off the west of England, the ancient Manx language is still sometimes used. In the Channel Islands a form of English is still common and in Cornwall in the extreme southwest of England attempts are being made to revive Cornish. Every region of the UK has its own accent and dialect, with words that are unique to one locality.

Immigrants have brought their own languages to Great Britain. The Jewish people brought many Yiddish words. Cantonese is spoken by Chinese from Hong Kong and Singapore, Urdu from Pakistan, Hindi from India and Bengali from Bangladesh are all heard in British cities.

The official religion of the UK is Anglican, a Protestant Christian religion governed by the Church of England. Other Anglican churches exist in Wales and Scotland. Scotland has its own church, the Church of Scotland, which is "Presbyterian." It is governed by a council of ministers and elders rather than by bishops.

After the establishment of the Church of England in 1527, Roman Catholicism was forbidden in Britain until 1829. However, it was secretly practiced. Around 14 percent of the population are Roman Catholics in Great Britain. Other Christian churches include the Baptists, the Methodists and the Greek Orthodox. Recently immigrant populations have introduced other religions such as Islam and Hinduism. There is a Jewish community in Britain for several centuries which now number about 300,000.

Each country of the United Kingdom has its own symbol. In England it is the rose. In Scotland, it is the thistle. In Wales it is the leek. In Northern Ireland it is a red hand.

The land of the British Isles was formed millions of years ago. The rocks of northwest Scotland are three billion years old. Volcanoes formed south to north indicating volcanic activity. The hill known as Arthur's Seat, on the outskirts of Edinburgh, is the remains of an extinct volcano. At the Giant's Causeway near Portrush, in Northern Ireland, dramatic hexagonal columns of rock emerge from the sea. They were formed from cool lava. The extensive sands on the northeast coast of Northern Ireland are evidence that the land was once tropical desert like the present Sahara. The big coalfields that lie under southeast Scotland,

England's northeast and the Midlands and South Wales were formed from the remains of giant, tropical ferns and trees.

Scotland was once joined to eastern Canada and it was volcanic activity that eventually separated the two. Around the same time, what is now southern England was covered by a vast, shallow sea, in which many generations of shellfish lived and died. Sludge emerged as chalk which now forms the cliff of Dover in southern England, as well as the "dows" (hills) that stretch westward as far as Wiltshire. In parts of this area prehistoric settlers carved figures into the ground; some of humans, some of animals, creating huge white forms in the green grassland.

During the Ice Ages ice covered Britain and the whole of northern Europe at least 3,000 feet thick with ice. In warmer periods huge glaciers gouged out valleys and lakes, forming the sea locks (Scottish for lake) on the west of Scotland and grinding great rocks into pebbles.

Some 2.5 million years ago, Britain was joined to Europe by a large, low-lying plain. As the ice melted the sea level rose, flooding this plain to form the North Sea and cutting off the British Isles from mainland Europe. Beneath the North Sea lie reserves of oil and natural gas.

The geography of the British mainland can be divided into lowlands and highlands. All the land to the south of Tyne River and city of Exeter is the lowland area. All of the land west and north, which includes Wales, Scotland and Northern Ireland, is the highland area. The lowlands are warmer than the highlands. The principal rivers flow through them and humidity can be relatively high.

Parts of the lowlands are actually below sea level. Five centuries ago there were 2,000 square miles of wet marsh and open water in the north of East Anglia between the cities of Cambridge and Lincoln. This area was known as The Fens. In the mid 17th Century, a Dutch engineer named Vermyyden was brought in to drain the land. He cut channels through the marshes and built embankments along them. He installed some 700 windmills to pump the water off the land. The windmills are long gone, replaced by mechanical pumps. Fertile "fenland" fields are 10 feet below the rivers that run through them.

The highest mountain in the United Kingdom is Ben Nevis in Scotland, which is 4,409 feet high. The second highest peak, Mount Snowdon, in Wales, is 3,560 feet high. The Pennine chain, described as the "backbone of England" reaches 2,930 feet at the highest northern point. In the Lake District in northwest England, Scafell Pike is 3,210 feet high. All of these areas have very dramatic scenery and are popular with walkers and attract large numbers of tourists. In Northern Ireland the highest point is Slieve Donart, at 2,786 feet. The most mountainous districts of Britain are easily accessible from the many roads that penetrate them.

ENGLAND

The country of England in the south of the British Isles is in every way the dominant region of the United Kingdom, both in terms of land area and population. 46 million people live in England. It is the center of the government, industry, finance and the international relations of the United Kingdom. The main urban area lies around London in the southeast. Birmingham is in the Midlands. Manchester and Liverpool are in the northwest. Newcastle is in the northeast.

The "Home Counties" is the name given to the group of counties that ring London in southeast England. They are Bedfordshire, Buckinghamshire, Herfordshire, Kent, East and West Sussex and Surrey. A "green belt" was established around London by law in the 1930s, an area in which further building of homes and factories was prohibited in order to contain the urban sprawl of the capital.

The Home Counties during the 1950s, which were intended to relieve population pressure in London and the suburbs, has only increased the number of workers who commute to London every day. There are still agricultural areas. Kent, with its fruit orchards, is known as "the garden of England." The Home Counties have become the most heavily populated region of the U.K.

The counties of Essex, Suffolk, Norfolk and Cambridgeshire make up East Anglia. The countryside is flat with only a few hills. It is a predominantly agricultural area, although there are numerous local industries. England's second to oldest university was established in the city of Cambridge in 1209 and has an international reputation for academic excellence.

The West County covers the counties of Dorset, Somerset, Devon, Cornwall, Wiltshire, Avon and Gloucestershire. Most of the West Country is agricultural. It is hilly and in places quite wild. Deer are common in rural areas of Exmoor in Devon and Dartmoor on the boundary between Devon and Cornwall. Dorset and Devon are lined with tourist resorts and Devon includes the balmy "English Riviera". The far western county of Cornwall is famous for its dramatic coastal scenery. It was one of the few remaining areas of Celtic culture after the Saxon invasion and for centuries was a center for copper and tin mining. The largest city in the West Country is Bristol, a major port.

The Midlands are in six counties called Worcestershire, Warwickshire, Staffordshire, Leicestershire, Nottinghamshire and Derbyshire make up the heartland of England. On the outskirts of this area lie the counties of Herefordshire, Shropshire, Lincolnshire, Northhamptonshire and Oxfordshire.

Most of the region is flat. The largest city in the Midlands is Birmingham, which became one of the country's principal manufacturing areas during the late 18th and early 19th centuries. It is still an important industrial and commercial center. The nearby city of Coventry has a substantial automobile industry. To the southwest is the Stratford-upon-Avon, the birthplace of William Shakespeare.

Oxford has a variety of smaller, high-tech industries, including computing and biotechnology. Oxford is the site of England's oldest university founded before the 12th Century whose buildings include one of the world's great libraries, the Bodleian. The colleges of Oxford contain some of the most beautiful of English architecture.

The Northwest are counties of Cheshire, Lancashire, Cumbria and Merseyside. Cheshire, with its rich agricultural land, has long been renowned as one of the wealthiest counties, but rural areas in the north soon give way to industry and commerce. The city of Liverpool on the Mersey River has been a leading port for much of its history. The building of the Manchester Ship Canal in 1894 linked inland Manchester to the sea. Manchester remains a major financial and industrial center, second only to London in its economic importance. The northern county of Cumbria borders Scotland and contains England's highest mountains. Cumbria also contains the Lake District with its mountains and spectacular Lakeland scenery.

The Northeast is made up of three counties known as Yorkshire, Durham and Northumberland. For centuries wool production from this region was one of England's most important trades. Clothing manufacture is still one of the principal industries in the region's southern cities. The coal that fueled the Industrial Revolution was partly mined in this region. Huge shipbuilding and engineering industries grew up around Newcastle-upon-Tyne. The upland areas of the northeast, which lie inland, are largely agricultural.

SCOTLAND

Scotland's two principal cities, Glasgow and Edinburgh are both in the lowlands and they have always been the country's centers of business and culture. The larger of the two cities, Glasgow, was once a major industrial capital. It is best known as a thriving cultural center. Edinburgh is the financial capital of Scotland and the seat of its parliament. Much of the land is agricultural to the north of the Forth River, which flows close to this city. There are small fishing ports.

The Grampian Mountains stretch from the west coast, north of Glasgow, to central Aberdeenshire, in the east. Agriculture is important there. Barley is produced. The discovery of oil and natural gas beneath the North Sea has brought new wealth to the area.

80 miles to the northeast of Aberdeen, the city of Inverness is known as the "capital of the Highlands." Inland a huge valley called Glen More runs southwestward to Fort William, on the west coast, splitting the Highlands in two. A canal was built in 1822 to link the inland lochs that line it. The largest of these is Loch Ness which is 20 miles long.

The west coast is deeply indented with lochs that open to the sea. Valuable fish farms have been established here. Inland the country is scarcely populated and there are very few roads.

Hundreds of islands lie off the west coast of Scotland. Close to the west coast are the Inner Hebrides, the largest of which is Skye. Farther to the west are the Outer Hebrides. The largest of these, Lewis, is divided into two. The smaller half is known as Harris and has given its name to the woolen tweed that has been made in the islands for centuries.

There are two groups of islands north of the mainland Scottish coast. The Orkneys are close to the Scottish mainland, while the remote Shetland Islands lie 80 miles farther north.

WALES

Much of Wales is mountainous except coastal areas to the south and west. Its industrial development has developed in the southeast becoming heavily populated. The coalfields of this region were once of great importance. Many of these mines have been closed.

The seaport city of Cardiff is the capital of Wales and its docks were once busy with the export of coal. Swansea, Wales' second city, lies 35 miles to the west. The rest of Wales is thinly populated. The Cambrian Mountains extend over much of its center. Sheep farming is an important source of income. Slate for roofs and floors is still mined. Anglesey is a large island off the western coast.

THE ISLE OF MAN

The Isle of Man is part of the British Isles in the Irish Sea between England and Ireland. It is a self-governing "dependency". It has its own parliament and legal system and it is not a member of the European Union. Its economy is based on tourism, agriculture and fishing. The capital is Douglas.

THE CHANNEL ISLANDS

The Channel Islands are Jersey, Guernsey, Alderney, Sark and several smaller islands. They are a dependency of the United Kingdom. These four principal islands have their own assemblies and courts of law. Jersey and Guerney issue their own currency and stamps. The islands lie close to the northern French coast at Normandy. A form of French is still used there in official proceedings. The climate is milder than that of mainland Britain and is ideal for raising spring flowers and vegetables early in the season and for cattle farming. The islands are also famous as a tax haven because of their low rates.

THE ISLAND OF SARK

The Island of Sark is a flat topped outcrop of rock surrounded by steep cliffs. It is a "fief", an estate held by permission of the English crown, and was granted that status by Queen Elizabeth I in 1565. The ancient laws state that no automobiles are allowed on this island. If police are needed they must be sent for from Guerney.

THE NATIONAL PARKS OF ENGLAND AND WALES

The National Parks Authority was set up in 1949 and the first parks were designated in the 1950s. The authority protects the natural beauty of important landscapes and provides employment for the local population. These parks are preserved because of care and conservation. Most of the parks are located in the western uplands of Britain. They include a wide variety of terrains from coastal areas to high mountains. Loch Lomond and the Trossachs in Scotland will be the next two national parks. Londoners enjoy most of the sun in the city's Regent's Park.

Names of parks in England are Northumberland, Lake District, Yorkshire, Dales, North Yorkshire, Moor, Peak District, Snowdonia, The Norfolk Broads, Breton Beacons, Pembrokeshire Coast, Exmoor, New Forest and Dartmoor. All these parks are open for the public to enjoy.

Fossil remains indicate that Britain's ancient past had crocodiles, elephants and rhinoceroses. Later, much of the British Isles was covered with dense forests, wolves, bears and wild boars. However, these animals have disappeared in the past 500 years.

SIGNIFICANT MOMENTS

Today, deer are the most common species in Great Britain. There are five species of deer in Britain. The red deer is the largest and the male has an impressive spread of antlers. It is most common in the Highlands of Scotland and on the moors of southwest England. There is a herd in Richmond Park on the western outskirts of Central London.

Other native species are the roe and fallow deer. The tiny muntjac from China has spread widely in southern England and the Chinese water deer, the only species without antlers, has established itself in East Anglia. Foxes are very common and use railroads to find their way into towns and cities where they scavenge food from garbage cans. Badgers and otters declined during the 20th Century. Otters have suffered because of their mink fur. Weasels, polecats and pine marten are still common. The polecat is restricted to Wales and the pine marten to Scotland and Northern Ireland.

Rabbits were once very common. Bats have greatly decreased in numbers. Bats are now legally protected as are all species of reptiles and amphibians. Shooting of wild ducks and geese and game birds is restricted to certain seasons and all other species are fully protected by law. The protection of birds of prey has been especially successful and the taking of eggs or young is strictly prohibited. The red kite is increasing in numbers in Wales. The golden eagle can be seen in Scotland and Northern Ireland. The nests of the asprey, or fish eagle are carefully guarded

BRITISH CITIES

LONDON, the capital of the UK, is Europe's largest city with a population of about eleven million people. London covers more than 600 square miles and it extends 30 miles. London was the most important city in the world in the 19th Century. Today London remains one of the world's major financial and cultural capitals.

London has more than 40 major theaters, two opera houses of international standing, three great concert halls and three leading resident orchestras. The Thames River flows from west to east across the city of London. Much of the city is made up of numerous former villages, each with its own distinct character, which have been joined up.

London is divided into 33 boroughs or political units, of which two are known as "cities"---the City of London and the City of Westminster. There are the St. Paul's Catholic Cathedral and the Tower of London which are prominent landmarks.

The City of Westminster is larger in area and includes many of London's most expensive residential districts such as Buckingham Palace where the queen and the royal family as well as the House of Parliament known as the "Palace of Westminster." Westminster Abbey was built in the 11th Century. It was redesigned over the next two centuries. Trafalgar Square was built to commemorate the naval victory against Napoleon. A statue of Admiral Horatio Nelson stands on a 164 foot tall column to the center of the square. The National Gallery lies along the north of the square.

To the west and north of Trafalgar Square is the West End, the main shopping and entertainment district. Most of London's major theaters are located in the West End such as the Royal Opera House. Oxford Street is the busiest shopping area. It is lined with department stores. Soho and Covet Gardens are lively areas with a huge variety of shops, restaurants, cafes and bards. Farther west are residential areas and green parkland such as Hyde Park, Kensington Gardens and Regent's Park.

EDINBURGH is Scotland's capital with a population of less than 500,000. It is the seat of its new-parliament. Edinburgh is the country's financial and cultural center. Edinburgh's main landmark is a castle, which rises on sheer cliffs above this city. King Malcolm III of Scotland first built a castle here in the 11th Century. The castle houses the chapel of St. Margaret, which is the city's oldest structure. A road known as the Royal Mile connects the Castle Rock with the palace of Hollyrood House. The 16th Century palace is the queen's official Scottish residence. The Royal Mile is a magnet for tourists and is lined with interesting shops, cafes and bars. Many important and impressive buildings lie on or close to the Royal Mile, including St. Giles cathedral, which dates from the late 14th Century. South of the Royal Mile is Edinburgh University.

SIGNIFICANT MOMENTS

The Edinburgh International Festival is held every August. It is one of the greatest art festivals in the world. Many visitors from around the world go to this festival. There are theaters, movies, art exhibits and dance performances. The Edinburgh Fringe Festival is held at the same time. Theater, dance and comedy shows are presented.

Edinburgh offers art and history such as the National Gallery of Scotland, the Scottish National Portrait gallery and the Royal Scottish museum. In July 1999, Scottish parliamentary elections were held for the first time in nearly 300 years. A new Parliament House is currently being built opposite Holyrood House. The magnificent Holyrood Park covers an area of 640 acres. Arthur's Seat is an extinct volcano that rises to 823 feet. There is a wonderful view from the top of this extinct volcano. The park has moorlands and lochs (lakes).

CARDIFF is the capital city of Wales and it is located in South Wales on the Bristol Channel. A Roman outpost was established on this site in about A.D. 75. It was occupied by Normans after their invasion of Britain in 1066. When the Glamorganshire Canal opened in 1794, Cardiff became an important seaport. Cardiff is an industrial center for the manufacturing of steel machinery and metal products, processed foods, textiles and paper.

The earliest remaining parts of Cardiff Castle, which is in the center of Cardiff, date from the 11th Century. Llandoff Cathedral on the outskirts of the city has been rebuilt and restored over the centuries. This cathedral dates from the 12th Century.

From the early 1990s, Cardiff has developed into the "fastest growing" capital city in Europe. There is a huge freshwater marina on Cardiff Bay in the south of the city with an opera house. This is a wonderful place to take a stroll on a sunny day. Buses go there from the city center. In 1988 the University College, Cardiff founded in 1883, was merged with the University of Wales Institute of Science and Technology, founded in 1866, to form the University of Wales College of Cardiff.

BELFAST is the capital city of Northern Ireland. It is a major port and industrial center. This city emerged as an important trading town in the 17th Century. Trade was greatly helped by the building of the Long Bridge over the Lagan River. The bridge was begun in 1682 and remained in use until the 1840s. It was replaced by the Queen's Bridge. In the 19th Century, industrial development, particularly in shipbuilding and linen, transformed the city from a small market town into a thriving industrial center. By 1842 Belfast's population had risen to 70,000. 20 years later it had a population of 120,000. At the centuries end it had reached 350,000.

When it officially became a city in 1888, Belfast was the largest commercial and industrial center, the chief shipbuilding center in Ireland. Belfast is the third-largest port in the United Kingdom (after London and Liverpool). There are many public buildings which include the City Hall of 1906. Musgrave Park was laid out in 1924. Ten years later the Museum and Art Gallery were opened and also in 1934 Belfast Castle and its grounds accepted visits by the public. Belfast's population in the 1950s was 450,000.

Among Belfast's main attractions today are the massive Odyssey Millennium Centre, the Golden Mile of restaurants, entertainment locales and pubs and the lively nightclubs around Queen's University.

IRELAND

All of us delight in the charm of the Irish people. We grew up on Irish folktales about fairies and leprechauns. The island of Ireland was ruled by Britain from 1169 to 1921. Today the people of the Republic of Ireland have finally achieved their dream.

Ireland is known for many shades of green in its landscapes. The name "Emerald Isle" has been used for green Ireland since the late eighteenth century. Ireland is known for its mystical beauty. There is mist lying in green valleys. Magnificent trees bend majestically in the wind off the coast. It is the home of the fairies, invisible creatures whom it isn't wise to anger. The rocks of ancient castles and churches seem to be held together by green ivy that now twines around them.

For 160 years, the Irish have been leaving the island to seek their fortunes in places with more jobs and opportunities. The population of the island had dropped from 8.5 million in 1840 to

2.8 million people. Many were living in poverty in this republic in the 1840s.

Even in the 1980s young people left Ireland to earn a living. High-tech computers began to be used in Ireland which has increased employment. Ireland's theaters, music, dance, folklore and literature are an important part of European and American culture.

The entire island of Ireland is 32,595 square miles in area. The Republic of Ireland is 27,126 square miles, which is about 83 percent of this island. Northern Ireland, a province of the United Kingdom, covers 5,459 square miles. The island is 302 miles at its greatest length and 171 miles at its greatest width.

Ireland is shaped like a saucer with a lowland area in the middle and mountains forming a raised outer edge. The mountains are not continuous. The mountains are covered with glaciers. Until the last great Ice Age, which ended about 10,000 years ago, Ireland and Great Britain were attached to the European continent. When the glaciers melted, the water level of the surrounding ocean rose enough to fill the low lying regions. Great Britain was separated from mainland Europe and Ireland from Great Britain. The Irish Sea lies between Ireland and Great Britain. The entire island of Ireland has a coastline of 3,500 miles. The lowest annual average temperature is 35 degrees F. The highest annual, average temperature is 61 degrees F.

Ireland is divided into four regions called Ulster, Munster, Leinster and Connacht (or Connaught). A fifth region called Meath is now regarded as part of Leinster. The old region of Ulster in the north consists of nine counties. This island has a jagged coast especially in the west, where the peninsulas jut out into the Atlantic. There is a series of three rugged and beautiful peninsulas on the southwest coast.

Iveragh, the center peninsula, is made famous by the Ring of Kerry. The ring is a beautiful, new road that circles the peninsula. Most tourists travel around the ring, which is 112 miles long. North of Iveragh and Dingle Bay is Dingle Peninsula. South of it is Beara Peninsula, which is much more rugged and isolated. South of Beara is Bantry Bay. Off each peninsula are small islands.

Most Irish children read Peig Sayer's book PEIG which tells about life on the island. The Blaskets are protected as a national park. The largest island lies off the coast of County Mayo known as Achill. Achill is 56 square miles and features cliffs, huge rocks and interesting moorlands.

The most famous islands are the three very isolated Aran Islands known as Irishmore, Irishmaan and Irisheer, which lie off Galway. Today, these islands can be reached by ferries or airplanes. Visitors are not allowed to bring cars with them.

North of Kerry is County Clare's rocky and spectacular coast. The Cliffs of Moher are a famous site in Ireland. For a distance of 5 miles the land ends in a sheer drop of 650 feet to the sea. Just inland from the cliffs is a limestone feature called the Burren. Its neighbor Connemara features beautiful sea cliffs, flower-filled bogs and charming lakes.

The Shannon is Ireland's longest river which is 240 miles. It exists in County Cavan, northwest of Dublin. In the eighteenth century the Grand Canal and the Royal Canal were built connecting Dublin to the Shannon. The lower Shannon is bordered by pastureland, making this an important dairy region. The Shannon widens at several places into lakes or boughs. The largest is Lough Derg. There are wetlands along the Shannon which attract many birds and other animals.

The largest lake in Ireland and in the British Isles is LoughNeagh, west of Belfast. It is 147 square miles in area, but seems even larger because it is surrounded by marshlands. Killary National Park was developed around Muckross House and Gardens. The spectacular scenery features Lough Leane, a popular lake for sailing, which is surrounded by mountains. Muckross House was built in the mid-1800s as a country estate. It was given to the nation, along with 11,000 acres. The park was later doubled in size.

The highest point in Ireland is Carrantouhill, at 3,414 feet. It is part of the range called Macgillicuddy's Reeks in Killarney. The mountains are named for Macgillicuddy, a man who once owned the mountains. Mount Brandon on Dingle Peninsula is the nation's second highest mountain. On St. Brendan's Day, May 16, people climb Mount Brandon along an ancient track called the Saint's Road.

SIGNIFICANT MOMENTS

Dubliners go hiking and have picnics at Wicklow Mountains. The Wicklow region south of Dublin is called the Garden of Ireland. The mountain of Mourne in County Down south of Newcastle in Northern Ireland are a group of low, rounded hills. A series of nine glens, or isolated valleys were created by the retreat of the glaciers long ago, as the waters ran off the northern end of the island. In the glens, the water still pours down in the form of waterfalls. The glens are surrounded by bogland and are hard to reach. Many Irish fairy tales tell of mystical events in the glens.

There are thirty-one species of mammals native to Ireland. There are the Irish hares, which are brown with white ears. Ireland once was the home of bears two hundred years ago. There are wolves, foxes, badgers, weasels, moles, martens and snakes in Ireland. Glenveagh National Park in the far north is home to a herd of red deer. Red deer have been moved onto the Blasket Islands. Some whales and sharks exist off the coast of Ireland. They can be seen from the Cliffs of Moher. Seals and sea lions lie on rocks along the coasts. Otters also live along the seacoast and they swim in the rivers.

Ireland has a hundred or more of its own bird species that nest on the island. A wildlife preserve in County Wexford is the winter home of three-quarters of the world's population of the Greenland, white-fronted goose. Ponies from Counemaree are the largest and the only pony native to Ireland.

Rathlin Island in Northern Ireland has only a few human inhabitants. However, it is home to thousands of graceful seabirds such as puffins, kittiwakes, razorbills, guillemots and ospreys. They nest in the area of southern Ireland called Eagle Rock. Ireland has only one reptile, a small lizard. Eels are substitutes for snakes. These long, thin fish which are great for eating, hatch in the North Atlantic. They swim across the oceans, heading for the rivers and streams of Ireland. Lough Neagh is known for its eel fishing.

Ireland has produced more breeds of dogs than any other country of its size. The Irish setter is a large, sleek dog with coppery, red hair. The Irish wolfhound is one of the largest dogs. When perched on its hind legs, it stands higher than a man. It weighs up to 200 pounds. The Irish and the Kerry blue terriers are energetic, small hunting dogs. The Irish water spaniel is a water loving dog. It is eager to dive into water to retrieve a bird for a hunter.

DUBLIN is the largest city in Ireland known for Irish trade, the largest population and for its cultured environment. It was fashionable for the English to have beautiful city homes in Dublin. Grafton Street connects St. Stephen's Green, a beautiful city park with Trinity College. Many fancy shops and businesses are located along this street. Parallel to it is Kildare Street where Leinster House, the National Museum and the National Library stand. Nearby is Mansion House, the residence of the Lord Mayor of Dublin. West of downtown Dublin is the Phoenix Park, which is the largest, fenced park in Europe. The zoo stands at the east end of this park. The official residence of the president of the Republic, called Aras, An Uachtarain, is in the park. It looks like the U.S. White House. The population is 986,000. The average temperature in Dublin is 40 degrees F. The average annual rainfall is 30 inches. "Molly Malone" is a folk song telling the tale of a Dublin woman who sells cockles and mussels on the streets of Dublin.

CORK is Ireland's second largest city located near the Lee River in southern Ireland. Cork is the major seaport of southern Ireland. Important industries in Cork include making leather goods, beer and spirits. University College in Cork attracts many students. Over 50,000 visitors attend the Cork Jazz Festival in October as well as the Cork Film Festival.

LIMERICK is the third largest city in Ireland, which is a seaport town on the Shannon River in southwestern Ireland. Limerick is known for its lace making, creameries and flour mills. This city's oldest building is St. Mary's cathedral founded in 1172. The Limerick Museum and the Hunt Museum provide Irish history for visitors to learn.

GALWAY is the fourth largest city. This western Ireland city is located northwest of Limerick on Galway Bay. University College at Galway is a center of Gaelic culture. Many college students study the Gaelic language. Many Irish people and visitors travel to Galway. There is a Jazz Festival in February. A Poetry and Literature Festival takes place in April. The Galway Film Festival and the Galway Race Week are in July

SIGNIFICANT MOMENTS

WATERFORD is the fifth largest city in Ireland which is located on the Suir River in southeastern parts of Ireland. It is an important port settled by the Vikings in the 700s. It is best known today for its beautiful Waterfront crystal. Many people tour the Waterford crystal factory and watch glassblowers, cutters and engravers as they make bowls, glasses and ornaments. Visitors also enjoy walking along this city's narrow streets and alleyways to see Christ Church Cathedral, Blackfriars Abbey and the Granary, which is a new museum.

You will enjoy the scenery, people, cities, coastal views and wild life in Great Britain. It is best to travel to Great Britain in late spring and during the summer.

TWENTY-EIGHT
CREATURES OF THE WORLD

Many creatures dwell in the world. Wildlife is abundant in the wilderness and country sides around the world. Wildlife needs a natural environment to live in. Forests, meadows, jungles and swamps are natural settings where living creatures dwell and survive.

Creatures of the Earth are mammals, reptiles, amphibians and ocean dwellers such as fish. Bears, mountain lions, cougars, wild goats, apes, monkeys, tigers, elephants, leopards, giraffes, zebras, panthers, anteaters, sloths and wild boars are creatures who live in the wildernesses. They must hunt for food and water in order to survive.

Many creatures have predators who chase after them because they are hungry and need food. Some creatures are carnivorous. Creatures who eat meat are lions, tigers, panthers, leopards, hyenas, wolves, coyotes, mountain lions, cougars and bears. Other animals are vegetarians such as elephants, giraffes, monkeys, apes, zebras, elks, deer, rabbits, antelopes and gazelles. Crocodiles and alligators eat meat.

More creatures are snakes, lizards, toads, turtles, rats, badgers, weasels, foxes, wild hares, owls, eagles, vultures, sheep, goats, cattle, dogs, cats, many types of birds and sealife such as whales, otters, seals, sharks, walruses, porpoises, octopi, squid, dolphins, water turtles and water snakes. All of these creatures must learn to survive on their own by finding food and shelter.

Survival of the fittest is what takes place in Nature. The weakest creatures usually do not survive long. They are captured and become food for their predators.

Creatures have existed on Earth for millions of years. They have instincts which help them learn to survive. Their survival instinct is important. Their environment is necessary in a natural setting so they can exist and dwell best in their natural environment.

Each creature eats certain food in their environment. It is necessary for each creature to adapt to the changing climate, environments, dry and wet environment, to predators, and sudden, dangerous experiences such as floods, severe earthquakes, tidal waves and severe droughts, etc.

Creatures who have long life spans have learned to stay alive by finding enough food, protective shelter and a healthy environment. Certain species have continued to live on Earth for millions of years. These species are elephants, snakes, lizards, horses, crocodiles, alligators, apes, monkeys and more.

Creatures on Earth help to maintain a natural ecosystem. They help to balance Nature on Earth.

TWENTY-NINE
WHY DO WE CRY?

W hy do we cry? Crying is an expression of our feelings of grief, sorrow and sadness. We cry to release our negative feelings about sudden shocks, injuries and loss of loved ones. We feel remorse and depression when unhappy events and situations take place in our lives.

Vanessa Swartz grew up in a family of six children. Her parents were immigrant Jews from Germany. They came to America during World War II to escape from the Nazi regime. Vanessa was 14 when her family left Germany in 1941. She felt sad because she had many friends in Germany in the neighborhood and schools where she grew up in Heidelberg.

Vanessa felt grief when her father was captured by the German Nazi Regime before her family left Germany. Her father, Bernard Swartz was tortured by Nazis because they suspected that he was a spy for England during World War II. He was taken from his home one night unexpectedly to be questioned by the Nazi investigators at the German Nazi Headquarters in Heidelberg.

Vanessa was close to both of her parents. She was the oldest child in the family. Vanessa's mother, Irm, was very upset when her husband, Bernard was suddenly forced to go in a Nazi car down to the Nazi Headquarters as a prisoner. Irm was afraid her husband would never return. She began crying because she didn't want to lose her husband.

Vanessa began crying because she loved her father. She didn't want him to be tortured by the Nazis. Vanessa and Irm prayed to Jehovah God to protect Bernard. However, they also cried and continued to cry because of their feelings about the injustice that had occurred regarding Bernard.

Irm, Vanessa and the other children prepared to escape from Germany. They didn't want to go to concentration camps devised by the Nazis. Many of their Jewish neighbors were taken away. They lived in fear and depredation day by day.

Several weeks went by and Bernard had not returned to his home in Heidelberg. Irma knew she must find a way to escape with her six children. She went underground to speak to Americans, who could help her. She told several American spies that her life was in danger as well as her children's lives. Several American agents arranged for Irm and her six children Vanessa, Mark, Herman, Michelle, Lisa and Cheryl to escape.

The Swartz family, except Bernard, escaped one day through an underground tunnel to a coastline American ship. They were hidden in rooms in this American ship. Irm, Vanessa and the other five children remained in these secret rooms. Food and water was brought to them day by day. There were seven single beds spread out in two rooms adjoining each other.

It took two weeks for the American ship to return to America. The Swartzs family hoped to begin a better life in America. They brought very little luggage because they were in a hurry to leave Germany. In fact, they were wearing the only clothes they had on. They only had German money which would have to be exchanged for American money.

The American ship had to navigate through dangerous waters in order to travel to America from the coast of England through the Pacific Ocean to New York City in America. The Swartz family waited day after day and night after night to reach America.

Irm and her six children were allowed to walk on deck after the American vessel was far away from Europe. If an alarm was sounded to warn them of danger they would return to their rooms below.

Finally the American ship arrived in New York Harbor. The ship passed the Statue of Liberty. The Swartz family gazed at the Statue of Liberty with amazement. They noticed the flame of liberty in the right hand of the Lady of Liberty. They spoke German and some English. Irm was able to read the message near the Statue of Liberty about freedom for all. She was impressed with this message about freedom and liberty for all.

Once the American ship was anchored in New York City Harbor the Swartz family was allowed to leave the ship. They were instructed to go to the Immigration section. They were carefully examined for diseases and for weapons. Obviously, they had no weapons. Fortunately, Irm and her six children were healthy enough to enter America. Irm declared that she did not believe in Hitler's Nazi Party. She stated that she was glad to be in America. She told the immigration officers that her husband had been forced to go to the German Nazi Headquarters. She explained that he never returned to their home. Irm had tears in her eyes. She began crying. The immigration officers understood her situation.

Irm Swartz and her children left the immigration office. They would need to find a place to stay in New York City. Irm was able to exchange German money for American money. She could read English. So, she purchased several newspapers to search for an apartment in New York City.

Finally, after circling several available apartments Irm called to find out the monthly rent for at least ten apartments. The rent ranged from $20 to $30 a month for 2 bedroom apartments in 1941. Irm only had $300 with her. This money would have to last until she had a job. She went to look at a $20 two bedroom apartment in The Bronx.

The two bedroom apartment was somewhat small. There were pieces of furniture in it. There were only two double beds. All the Swartz's would have to share these two beds. The boys were asked to sleep in bedrolls on the floor. Three girls would sleep in a double bed. Irm and Vanessa slept in the other bed.

As soon as the Swartz family was settled in their new apartment, Mrs. Swartz went looking for a job as a maid. Vanessa looked after her younger sisters and brothers. Irm Swartz waited several weeks before she was offered a position as a maid in someone's home in Manhattan. The monthly salary was only $50. The Swartz family would have to live on this small income. Groceries cost at least $20 a month. By the time the rent and groceries were paid for, there was only $10 left for other things. It cost Irm 5 cents a day to go by bus back and forth to her apartment. She worked six days a week from 8 a.m. until 7:30 p.m. for her small salary of $50 a month.

Irm purchased a used, sewing machine. She bought inexpensive fabric and thread. She made clothes for her children and herself. Her children were kept clean and they wore their new clothes. Vanessa and Irm knitted warm, woolen sweaters for all the children to wear. Irm knitted a warm sweater for herself. She wore a scarf around her head, especially on rainy days.

The children needed new shoes to wear to school. Shoes cost 75 cents each. Irm managed to spend $4.50 for six pairs of leather shoes for six children. She wore old shoes she brought from Germany in order to save money. She only had $75 left of her savings by the time she found a job as a maid.

The Swartz children all attended the nearest schools to their new home. Vanessa, 14, attended high school. Mark, 13, attended eighth grade. Herman, 11, attended grade six. Michelle, 10, attended grade five. Lisa, 9, attended grade four. Cheryl, 7, attended grade two. Michelle, Lisa and Cheryl attended elementary school. Mark and Herman attended junior high school.

The three schools were within walking distance. During warmer days all of the children walked to school. On rainy and snowy days they went to school and came back home on public buses. The children were required to speak English in school. All school work was in the English language. The Swartz children learned to complete their daily assignments. They learned to speak English and write in the English language.

Irm Swartz continued to work as a maid for a wealthy couple in Manhattan. She scrubbed floors, washed dishes, did the laundry, made beds, dusted and vacuumed the house and helped prepare breakfast, lunch and dinner six days a week.

Irm was tired at the end of her work day. She took a public bus home.

When Irm Swartz returned to her residence she laid down to rest. It was 8:30 p.m. by the time she walked into her apartment. Vanessa was helping her sisters with their homework. Mark and Herman helped wash and dry the dinner dishes. Vanessa had cooked the dinner. Irm came into the small dining room at the corner of the small kitchen to eat her dinner after she had rested for awhile. She visited with Vanessa, Mark and Herman. The younger girls had gone to bed at 9:15 p.m. Irm reminisced about her work day. Vanessa, Mark and Herman spoke about their experiences at school and in their new neighborhood.

Irm was grateful that her children and she were safe in New York City. They all had an opportunity to live a better life there. Irm still cried in her bedroom at night because she missed her husband, Bernard. She felt sad that he was unable to be with her and their children. Vanessa and the other children missed their father. Yet, they went on with their new lives in America.

THIRTY
USES OF GLASS

There are many uses of glass. Glass is made from melted sand. When the sand is liquified it can be formed in molds to produce glass objects.

Drinking glasses, cups, saucers, plates, cooking casserole dishes, vases, pitchers, salt and pepper shakers and glass menageries for displays are made from glass. Glass must harden in the shapes they are designed to become.

Glass can break. So glass objects must be handled carefully. Objects made of plastic and metal do not break. However, glass objects can sparkle and they can be washed easily and readily. Glasses for drinking and glass plates, cups and saucers can be decorated with various designs. They look attractive when they are designed.

Glass menageries such as birds, angels, bells, animals and flowers made with glass are very interesting to look at. Many glass objects such as vases, pitchers, animals and plants made of glass can be displayed on shelves in one's living room, dining room and kitchen.

Glass has been produced for many centuries. It is a useful substance which can be used to make many things. Even porcelain glass dolls are made out of glass.

Glass will probably continue to be used for many years. Glass is produced in factories. Glass-blowing is popular in Europe and America.

THIRTY-ONE
ENJOY THE CARIBBEAN ISLANDS

With its endless beaches, swaying palm trees, pleasant climate and friendly islanders the Caribbean Islands live up to its name. There are volcanic mountains and lush rain forests in the Caribbean Islands.

Haiti is one of the most beautiful, Caribbean Islands. Sugarcane flourishes on many of the islands. It was introduced from the Mediterranean by Spanish colonists. There are other crops such as bananas, citrus fruits and coffee beans as well as animals (cattle, dogs and horses which came from Asia and Europe).

Cities, towns and villages bear the imprint of former colonial powers. The Spaniards built Havana, with its colonnades and plazas. The British built Bridgetown with its Victorian architecture and "tropical Anglican" cathedral.

Different histories have influenced the formerly Spanish colonies of Cuba, Puerto Rico and the Dominican Republic. Sugar plantations stretch across these islands for 500 years. European influence is still prevalent in Martinique and Guadeloupe. The Dutch style of Curacao or Aruba has gabled pastel warehouses lining the canal and port to conjure up a tropical Amsterdam.

Britain has left its mark of colonial rule in its former possessions, red postboxes, English place names and cricket
fields.

The original, indigenous population of the Caribbean disappeared within half a century. People have come from around the world to live in the Caribbean Islands. The original Arawak people did not survive. Europeans conquered, colonized and recreated the Caribbean in their own image. The Spanish language has become the dominant speaking language. The great majority of Caribbean people come from Africa. West African Ashanti dialect is spoken. African speech and customs are commonplace in Haiti and around the eastern tip of Cuba. 40 percent of the population of Trinidad is East Indian in origin. The stores and restaurants of Port of Spain, the capital, are filled with sounds, sights and scents of the Indian subcontinent from sari shops to street traders. Many Hindu prayer flags surround many countryside homes.

Haiti and the Dominican Republic are among the world's poorest, while Puerto Rico, Trinidad and the Virgin Islands enjoy some prosperity. Economic hardship has influenced many people to leave the Caribbean's poorest countries to live and work in North America and Europe. Possibly one in seven Dominicans live in the U.S.A. In the 1950s nearly 10 percent of all Jamaicans immigrated to Britain. Both English, French and Spanish are spoken in the Caribbean Islands.

The marketplace is the traditional center of Caribbean social and economic life. By bus or on foot, the market women arrive before dawn to set up their displays of fresh fruit and vegetables. The market is set up usually in the town square or at the rural crossroads which is mostly run by females. There are many tubers, bunches of green bananas and plantains, red-hot peppers, tangy limes and enormous avocados. Most people usually have a small piece of land to grow fruit trees and vegetables. Even though, there is much poverty, few actually go hungry.

The Caribbean Islands are still a largely agricultural region. Important changes are taking place in what crops are grown and where they go. From the earliest colonial days, the region was an exporter of agricultural commodities such as sugar and created more wealth than the whole of the British Empire.

The advent of European sugar, sugar beet, global overpopulation and changing diets have long since undermined the Caribbean sugar industry.

Lobster, red snapper and flying fish are found on restaurant menus throughout the Caribbean Islands. However, the Caribbean Sea cannot withstand intensive fishing.

High in the hills of Haiti, animal sacrifices, rhythmic drumbeats and colorful dancers swirl around a crackling bonfire which are all part of the island's most famous and mysterious religious voodoo. There are mosques in Trinidad, Hindu temples in Guyana and pilgrimage sites in the Dominican Republic. Jews, Muslims and Hindus exist in the Caribbean Islands. Many Caribbean people are Christians. European colonizers brought different Christian beliefs to the Caribbean Islands. Catholicism is the main faith of Haiti and the Dominican Republic. The influence of U.S. Protestant beliefs have spread around the Caribbean Islands. Africans had their own beliefs. Each village has its churches with a variety of religious beliefs. Over time these beliefs merged with Christian religion to create new forms of faith and ceremony. Haitians are 90 percent Christian and 100 percent voodooist.

Rastafarianism has its roots in Jamaica. Rastafarianism expresses many people's longing for an African identity by invoking Ethiopia as the holy land and the late Emperor Haile Selassie as a god and promotes the smoking of marijuana as a sacrament.

The British promoted the Westminster model of parliamentary democracy and all English speaking islands hold regular elections. The Spanish islands, meanwhile, have adopted a presidential system with a greater tradition of "strong man" leadership.

Most independent Caribbean territories have a multi-party electoral system government. Elections are fiercely contested events and can lead to violence. On small islands personalities are often as important as policies especially when most electors know the candidates personally. Most states are proud of their constitutional credentials.

Of all the Caribbean territories only two are generally agreed to have undemocratic governments. Cuba has been dominated by Fidel Castro and the Communist Party since the 1959 revolution. It has alienated the USA by refusing to hold free elections. Cuba has become increasingly isolated. Economically strangled by the US embargo, Cuba suffers a shortage of basic goods. It is a popular tourist destination for Europeans, Canadians and Latin Americans, who bring money into Cuba.

Tourism has brought prosperity to the Caribbean Islands. Tourist earnings far outweigh exports even in larger and more prosperous islands such as Jamaica and Barbados. Economists believe that more jobs have been created because of tourism.

Every island produces rum, ranging from mass-market brands to local firewater. The best way to sample the better rums is with ice and lime juice, the basis of the classic Planter's Punch cocktail. Each Caribbean island claims to make the best rum. The best rums are from Cuba, Haiti, Jamaica, Martinique and Barbados.

The islands of Grenada, St. Lucia, Dominica and St. Vincent are covered with volcanic peaks and fringed with beautiful beaches. The four Windward Islands lie facing the Trade winds head on---on a line of jagged, volcanic protrusions, some still active and liable to erupt about once every 100 years.

Peaceful Arawak islanders were decimated by invading Caribs in about A.D. 1000. Five centuries later the Caribs were defending themselves against European colonists. In 1748 Dominica was left to the Caribs in the Treaty of Aix-la-Chapelle. The Windward Islands finally were taken over by the British. They became a Crown Colony in 1874 administered from Grenada. The islands all gained their independence from Britain in the 1970s. Yet, they remain within the Commonwealth and they still use the British judicial system.

DOMINICA

Dominica claims to have a river for every day of the year. Dominica has lush, green volcanoes with spectacular scenery and interesting coastal villages. At 29 miles by 16 miles Dominica is the largest of the Windwards. Many islanders fish for a living.

SIGNIFICANT MOMENTS

This was a Carib stronghold for hundreds of years. Dominica has made money from coffee and sugar. British and French colonies were established here.

Dominica is located between the French islands Martinique and Guadeloupe. Dominica had strategic value for France and it has retained a strong French heritage. Many of the 71,000 Dominicans are Roman Catholics and Creole speakers.

Dominica's capital, Roseau, lies in the southwest of the island. It is a small, working town of about 20,000 people, with a mixture of modern buildings and interesting stone and wooden Victorian townhouses. In the oldest part is Dawhiney Market Square, now the site of a craft market, tourist information center and the Dominica Museum which has information descriptions of island life from colonial times to the presenting pictures and exhibits which includes volcanic geology.

The new market is at the end of the Bay Front. The Catholic Cathedral north of the old market site, stands out. Not far from there is Fort Young which is now a hotel. The real beauty of Dominica is on the outskirts of town. Botanical Gardens exist with 150 species of plants and Dominica parrots. At the head are the Papillate Wilderness Retreat and three waterfalls called the Trafalgar Falls.

The village of Laudat is the entry point to the scenic Moren Trails Pitons National Park, which received its name from a mountain peak. Adventurous hikers might want to hike to the Valley of Desolation, an area of bubbling pools and mud ponds and the Boiling Lake, a crater of steaming water that can boil an egg in three minutes. Near the pinnacles caves and drop-offs, a freshwater spring fizzles at truly scolding temperatures.

The road inland from Canefield climbs into the rain forest and mountains, touching the northern limits of the National Park which gives access to Middleham Falls and the Emerald Pool and waterfall. There are good spots for swimming on the Layou River along the Caribbean Coast. You can see colorful parrots in the Northern Forest Reserve.

Portsmouth is the island's second town. It is quieter than Rosau. Canoe trips are arranged here to take passengers through the Indian River mangroves. Cabrits National Park is on old military garrison. Many of the barrack buildings have been repaired and there is a museum in Fort Shirley. The park includes a marine section with scuba diving sites. Portsmouth's black sand beaches exist. Dominica's best beaches are to the east in the hidden north coast coves such as Hampstead or Califishie. Swimmers should be aware of the Atlantic swells.

Rivers were once gathering places to wash clothes and to socialize. Rivers play an important part in Caribbean folklore and legend. The Windward Islands have a lot of water. So, they sell water to other drier islands.

On Dominica, hunting parties search the rivers by night for frogs and crabs. Hunters used flaming torches. Today flashlights are used. Wild animals are startled by the light. They can easily be picked up by hunters.

GRENADA

Grenada has become a sleepy island. St. George is a picturesque port. It is a warm, friendly place of small villages. Rum punch is produced on Grenada. Many spices grow in Grenada such as nutmeg, cinnamon, coca, cloves, pimento and bay leaves.

Grenada is the most southerly in the chain of the Windward Islands. Of the Grenadines its string of offshore islets is surrounded by coral reefs, Carracou and Petit Martinique.

St. George's Grenada's capital is a very pretty town on a natural harbor. Georgian stone houses and more recent concrete homes are neatly arranged in curved lines on the crumbled slopes of a long-inactive volcanic crater, their red tiled and tin roofs offset by the tropical greens of the surrounding forest. Grenada gained independence in 1974 from Britain.

THE GRENADINES

The Grenadines appeal to adventurous singles and couples who like to go sailing, enjoy sports, gambling or go shopping. Hotels are small. The food is simple and there is a peaceful laid-back atmosphere. The 32 islands and cays that make up the lush and mountainous Grenadines offer numerous unspoiled white sand bays and coves as well as snorkeling, hiking, sailing and swimming. Just off St. Vincent, Young Island, is a private resort with only about 20 cottages. Bequic lies 8.5 miles south of St. Vincent. This is an island of fisherman, seafarers, boat builders and whalers. Tourism is popular here. The best places to stay include Frangipani and the Friendship Bay Hotel on the south coast. You can reach the excellent beaches of Princess Margaret Beach and Lower Bay by water taxi, or walk over to the secluded sand at Industry Bay in the east.

ST. LUCIA

The lively pulse of local soca, Martinique yourk and Jamaican reggae can be heard at St. Lucia's Rodney Bay. The mixture of people at Gros Islet is typical of St. Lucia. Tourism is concentrated in the northwest between the capital, Castries and the northern tip of this island where the best beaches exist.

Most St. Lucians are friendly. They speak patois, a Creole language derived mainly from French. However, English is the official language. St. Lucia was a British colony for one-and-a-half centuries until independence on the 22nd of December, 1979. St. Lucia is the most populous because there are 156,000 islanders. It is the most developed of the Windward Islands.

Castries, St. Lucia's capital, was named for a French Minister of the Marine, the Marechal de Castries. There are 62,000 people in Castries. Traditional Caribbean architecture survives on the hills around town, on Vigie Point and Moren Fortune.

The main square in the center of town has been renamed for one of St. Lucia's Nobel Prize winners, Derek Walcott. It is dominated by a huge saman tree and the brick Cathedral of the Immaculate Conception built in 1897. On the south side are a number of old Creole, timber-frame houses. A short walk away, Castries life is at its most ebullient in the market all along the waterfront in the tin-roofed vegetable market and in the craft market.

Rodney Bay has been the center for sailing craft and beach bards, popular with locals especially on weekends. Before the gin joints came Carib canoes, Spanish galleons, pirates' ships and naval ships. Two centuries ago Admiral Rodney fortified Pigeon Island National Park across the bay from Reduit Beach.

There is one 18-hole golf course among the chic villas of the Cap Estate farther north and a nine-hole course at La Toc, south of Castries.

Other places to go to in St. Lucia is Marigot Bay, a steep-sided inlet lined with palm trees, which was once a hideout for pirates and navies. There are a couple of cafes on the roadside down to the bay. At Canaries the coast road turns inland and goes to a rain forest.

Soufriere is the world's only drive-in volcano which is a simmering cauldron of mud that can be tracked down by its odor. Inland from Soufriere is the Diamond Botanical Gardens and Mineral Baths. At the Morne Coubaril Estate you can see cocoa-making, go hiking and horseback riding. You can continue to St. Lucia National Rain Forest.

ST. VINCENT

St. Vincent is a fertile and beautiful island from the cultivated valleys to the rain forested slopes of its active volcano. Its rigged east coast and fascinating Arawak settlement are worth seeing. There is also first rate diving and snorkeling as well as hiking on trails as verdant as any in Hawaii.

The 11,000 Vincentians are mainly of African origin, the descendants of plantation slaves. St. Vincent was one of the last strongholds of the Carib people. The British took over St. Vincent and built up a trade of sugar and cotton. Independence was gained in 1879. Agriculture still provides much of the island's living. Exports include arrowroot starch, bananas, and coconuts.

The capital of St. Vincent and the Grenadines is Kingstown, which is a few streets of Georgian townhouses with cobbled, orchid walkways set on a wide southwestern bay. There is a neo-Gothic and Romanesque Roman Catholic Church which was built in 1823. Away from the waterfront the ground rises throughout lying suburbs to the range of hills surrounding the town. In the northwest are the 20 acres of the St. Vincent Botanic Gardens dating back to 1763. There are sealing wax palms, red hot cat tail and roucou used in body paint by the Carib tribes.

SIGNIFICANT MOMENTS

There are rain forest trails in the Buccament Valley. Boats will sail from Kingstown to the Falls of Baleine, a cascade into a rock pool at the island's northern tip past the villages of the leeward shore.

THE LEEWARD ISLANDS

The Leeward Islands has a vast choice of beaches, friendly, small towns and varied, local customs. English is the primary language spoken. Antigua is the most developed vacation island. The six Leeward Islands lie in tow lines. To the west, Montserrat, Nevis and St. Kitts are the rain-forested peaks of a relatively young, volcanic chain (about 15 million years old). Antigua and Barbuda are to the east. Anguilla is the most northerly of the Lesser Antilles. Capped with coral limestone, the Lesser Antilles have some of the finest sand in the Caribbean.

The islands of Antigua and Barbuda established their full independence from Britain in the 1980s. St. Kitts and Nevis remain as a British Commonwealth. Montserrat and Anguilla are still British Overseas Territories. British settlers first arrived at St. Kitts in 1623. England and France disputed over this land. The British colonized with slave laborers to plant and harvest sugar cane. Eventually the slaves were freed. They scraped a poor living from subsistence farming. Today you will still see subsistence farmers living on the Leeward Islands.

The more developed islands, Antigua and Anguilla, tend to have better restaurants. A stroll around Nevis or a visit to the rum stores will give a taste of local life. Each island offers special features. The people of Anguilla and Barbuda have a reputation for a proud and independent outlook. All Leeward Islanders are known for their easy-going attitude. Anguilla offers some of the best restaurants and beaches in the Caribbean. There are at least 30 tiny, secluded coves, snorkeling beaches and walking areas all with fine sand with a view of a turquoise sea. There are no buses on this island. Taxis will pick tourists up at the airport, from the Blowing Point ferry dock, or from hotels. Its chic and expensive hotels are a second home to film stars and executives seeking a retreat from the humdrum. Those wanting nightlife and shopping can always sneak over to Sinte Maarten.

Most hotels have watersports facilities. Barnes Bay is a strip of sand backed with rocks and broad-leaved sea grape trees. Mead's Bay has a lovely sunset view from the Malliouhaue end. Calm and protected Road Bay harbors local boats and some larger ships and has a variety of restaurants. Just beyond Cracus Bay is Little Bay. Limestone Bay and Shoal Bay have fine sand, a watersports concession and snorkeling offshore. On the north coast lies Captain's Bay, a half moon of secluded sand. Rendevous Bay is a mangrove and dune-backed walking area with a clear view of Saint-Martin and a shipwrecked galleon, The Dune. The Moorish domes of the Cap Juluca Hotel overlook crescent-shaped Maunday's Bay. Shoal Bay West is overlooked by the tall, white curves of the Cove castles hotel villas. Sandy Island and Prickly Pear Cays have fine beaches and are good for a day's sailing trip. One departs from Island Harbour for the spit of land called Scilly Cay, famed for its grilled lobster and beach party atmosphere.

The territory of Antigua and Barbuda actually consists of three islands. Antigua is the main island at 108 square miles with excellent beaches. 66,000 people live there. Barbuda is a smaller, wooded island to the north with a population of 1,100. Redonda is a small uninhabited rocky islet lying 25 miles southwest of Antigua.

In Antigua, Redcliffe Quay has restored warehouses and townhouses occupied by stores and cafes. The Old Court House of the island now has the Anetigua and Barbuda Museum. St. John's Cathedral is a towering building from 1848 close to the Recreation Ground where international cricket matches have been hosted here since Antigua and Barbuda became independent in 1981. St. John's Public Market, south of town, is liveliest on Saturday mornings. Antigua's main tourist areas are to the west of the capital on the beaches of Five Islands Peninsula and to the northern Runaway and Dickenson Bays. From here the road follows the coastline north through interesting residential areas and past secluded coves to VC Bird International Airport and the Cedar Valley Golf Club.

The 200 year old plantation estate of Betty Hope, to the west, has been restored with a renovated windmill. In another windmill on the southeast coast is the Harmony Hall gallery which sells good quality Caribbean arts and crafts.

Corals, sponges and shellfish exist in the Leeward Islands. Sponges and anemones add their own color and variety to the marine world. Around a thousand species of fish live in the Caribbean Sea. There are angelfish, butterfly fish, Damsel fish, wrasses, predatory fish and parrotfish, etc.

There is a frigate bird sanctuary in Barbuda. Caves exist in the northeast with Indian rock carvings and River Fort, which is a Martello tower on the south coast.

Montserrat is a self-styled Emerald Isle with lush green hills, fertile valleys and volcanic sand beaches. Soufriere Hills volcano rumbled into action in 1995. Montserratians are trying to rebuild their tourist industry. The Irish gave the name Montserrat to this island. St. Patrick's Day is celebrated and the island's stamps feature an Irish harp. Montserrat Volcano Observatory houses scientists monitoring the island's volcanic activity. Visitors can tour the observatory with a guide and watch videos of volcanic action. Other activities include boat rides with views of Plymouth and other ruined settlements, sports fishing, hiking and bird watching in the Silver and Centre Hills with the Montserrat Forest Rangers.

At present Montserrat entire population has reduced from 11,000 prior to the 1995 volcanic eruptions down to 4,000. Visitors will find the handful of hotels, restaurants and businesses at the northern portion of the island.

The small volcanic island of Nevis lies between St. Kitts, across a strait called the Narrow and Montserrat. It is almost circular---just 5.5 miles by 8 miles and rises to the central peak of 3,232 feet. Nowadays, life for the 10,000 Nevisians is gentle and the grandeur of the islands' past, when it was known as the "Queen of the Caribbean" has disappeared, but the island is proud of its beautiful, restored plantation houses, which is where many visitors stay. The island's capital is Charlestown, a small collection of stone and timber frame houses laid out on the leeward coast. Inland from the waterfront is Memorial Square, a triangular park with banks and stores. Nearby are the Court House and Library as well as a small tourist office. At the northern end of town is the Museum of Nevis History.

Other attractions are Pinney's Beach, Fort Charles, Bath Estate, Nelson's Museum, Fig Tree Church and the Botanical Gardens of Nevis. St. Kitts (St. Christopher) had vast tracts of bright green sugar cane swaying in the breeze and estate houses standing aloof in colonial elegance. This island's southeastern peninsula has golden sand beaches. St.Kitts is shaped like a paddle with forest clad mountains and an old volcanic crater occupying the blade. St. Kitts became a rich plantation island. Brimstone Hill is one of the biggest forts in the Caribbean. Poinciana trees grow all over St. Kitts Island.

Basseterre is the island's capital. It was built on the protected Caribbean coast. Basseterre is a French name. The Circus is an open traffic circle overlooked by stone buildings with elegant balconies, a colonial chocktower and the Berkeley Memorial which is at its center. Spencer Cameron Art Gallery displays local and expatriate Caribbean works of art. A Catholic cathedral of the Immaculate Conception has twin spires and a magnificent rose window.

There are accommodations, a golf course and a popular beach in Frigate Bay while Friar's Bay over the next hill, has a marvelous beach of soft golden sand, which gets busy as soon as cruise ships arrive. A rollercoaster peninsular road leads up and down hill and past the salt ponds. The southern beaches have superb views across the narrows to Nevis. Old Road Bay marks the site of the first British settlement and was the capital until 1727. Amerindian rock carvings can be seen on

the Wingfield Estate nearby Romney Manor, a 17th Century great house set in tropical gardens, is the home of Caribelle Batik, a store selling silk-screened prints and clothes. You can watch island women practicing the art of batik.

Black Rocks are an interesting form of volcanic lava. From here the road leads south along the wild Atlantic coast passing through quiet villages and returning to Basseterre via the airport. The sugar cane factory is open to visitors between January and June.

THE VIRGIN ISLANDS

The U.S. and British Virgin Islands are worlds apart. The U.S. islands of St. Thomas and St. Croix have more in the way of attractions and entertainment. There is sailing and watersports. Visitors go to St. John. The Virgin Islands are green and they have peaks of a submerged chain of volcanoes. There are 90 islands. In the west are the three main United States Virgin Islands. St. Thomas, St. John, St. Croix, Tortula and Virgin Gorda exist within miles from each other.

Today, the U.S. Virgin Islands offer all the expected American comforts and conveniences with a tropical setting and Caribbean atmosphere. The banks are American as well as the fast food places. American currency is used. There are supermarkets and islanders play baseball.

St. Thomas is very developed and crowded. It has wonderful shopping in Charlotte Amalie and interesting restaurants. The third island and the largest of the Virgin Islands is St. Croix which has a variety of beach hotels, restaurants and interesting town buildings in Christiansted and Frederiksted. St. Croix's first casino opened in 1998. There are several good golf courses. Approximately 150,000 tourists visit the Virgin Islands annually.

Tortola is the hub of yachting. There is transportation by ferry to many other islands including Virgin Gorda, with top-rank accommodations, secluded beaches and offshore cays. Tortola has a scrubby and meandering spine of steep mountains rising to 1,709 feet at Mount Sage. The main settlement is Road Town, a modern capital made up of a few streets near a deep bay in the southern coastline. Tortolans live in small settlements on the coast. Transportation around the island is customarily by taxi or rented car. The best bays and beaches are on the island's side. At the West End, where most of the hotels are, you will find waterside pubs and stores, at the Soper's Hale Marina complex and the main ferry terminal. Smuggler's Cove is an isolated curve of sand. Heading east you come to Long Bay, where surfers enjoy the big waves. The long and lovely Cane Garden Bay has small places to stay and a variety of excellent beach bars and restaurants. East of Road Town there are good beaches here including Joshian's Bay and Long Bay on Beef Island. The Last Resort is a lively restaurant and bard on an island in Trellis Bay. You can spend the day on Marina Cay, which has good water sport. There is a free ferry.

Virgin Gorda has resorts hidden in its coves and offshore cays. Lawrence Rockefeller built the Little Dix Bay Hotel here. Virgin Gorda looks like a reclining woman. Its 8 square mile area is divided into three mounds and covered in scrub and cactus, rising to a 1,358 foot peak in the north. Granite boulders form The Baths which are a maze of water filled caves.

The road to the north of the islands passes isolated coves such as Savannah Bay and Pond Bay before reaching Virgin Gorda's second town, Gun Creek. This overlooks the North Sound, a stretch of water surrounded by tall peaks, cays and small islands with fine beaches. Two splendid hotels lie at this end of the island with fine beaches, accessible only by boat from Gun Creek. Biras Creek is a place of beauty overlooking a bay with a main beach and wild Atlantic surf. You can eat at The Restaurant in Leverick Bay, an elegant restaurant, at Drake's Anchorage on Mosquito Island, at a beach bar on Prickly Pear Cay and the tiny Saba Rock, "a bar that wakes up in the evening."

Sir Frances Drake Channel is the sailing heartland of the Virgin Islands, which is a magnificent stretch of water off Tortola where the white triangles of yacht sails beat back and forth over a beautiful blue sea. Fallen Jerusalem and Round Rock lie off Virgin Gorda, which has become a national park. Ginger Island is uninhabited. Cooper Island has about 10 inhabitants. Salt Island takes its name from a salt pond that is still formed. This is one of the Virgin Island's most popular dive sites with the wreck of the RMS Rhone which sank in the 19th Century lying offshore. Peter Island has one island resort with rooms spread out with views of the bay. Normal Island is the last island in the chain and is also uninhabited. It is worth visiting to see the water bound caves at Treasure Point. You can snorkel and go kayaking here.

St. Croix is the largest of the Virgin Islands and lies 31 miles to the south of the main U.S. Virgin Islands group. St. Croix has attractive harbor towns. It is twice the size of St. Thomas and it is sparsely populated with mountains, rain forest, beaches, dairy and cattle-breeding farmlands.

St. Croix's main town is Christianstad on the waterfront in the east. Fort Christiansvaern was an old defense in the town.

SIGNIFICANT MOMENTS

The Old Customs House and the Scale House is near the wharf. The Steeple Building is a museum of Native American artifacts. King Street Government House still houses government offices. The downtown has become a National Historic Site preserving several blocks for future generations.

Centerline Road heads west toward Frederiksted through agricultural land that made St. Croix wealthy during the 19th Century. The St. George Village Botanical Garden is a peaceful retreat on an old plantation estate, growing Amerindian and other Cruzian plants. There is the Cruzan Rum Factory off the main road. The Whim Great House is an unusual rounded estate building restored with colonial style antiques. There is sugar machinery displayed here. There are more colonnaded trading buildings in Frederiksted which includes restored Fort Frederik and its museum. Mahogany Road leads northward through rain forests.

St. John is one of the most beautiful islands in the Caribbean. St. John is the smallest and least developed of the U.S. Virgin Islands. It is a few miles east of St. Thomas, which is a short ferry ride across the Pillsbury sound. Approximately two-thirds of the island are given over to the Virgin Islands National Park. So, most of its steep, volcanic hills are left to grow a natural jungle. There are numerous trails through the park, on foot, on horseback and underwater through the corals of Trunk Bay with hikes and activities led by well informed rangers.

You can see ruins of the Annaberg Plantation, a relic of Danish days when the island was covered with sugar cane. Around the fringes of the National Park, St. John's coastline has been developed. Cruz Bay, at the western tip of the island, is the main town. There are many restaurants as well as the Elaine Jone Sprauve Library and Museum with marine life displays and artifacts dating from a slave revolt against Danish planters in 1733.

St. Thomas is the U.S. V.I. capital island and the most developed of all the Virgins. It is mountainous and has a population of over 50,000 people. It has excellent restaurants, clubs and bars near Charlotte Amalle. Ferries arrive at this downtown waterfront. Many tourists head for Havensight Mall, the first of the island's shopping centers which has been converted from a series of warehouses. Safari buses and taxis provide transportation for passengers from here into town. St. Thomas Skyride provides visitors with a 7 minute, 700 foot lift to a spectacular viewpoint overlooking the town and bay. St. Croix can be seen across the bay on a clear day. Charlotte Amalie's old trading streets are in unusual patterns with narrow alleys with restaurants and stores along the waterfront. You will pass the light green Virgin Islands Legislature Building that was built in 1874 by Dana as a police barracks and is now the USVI Senate.

Across the road is the dark red and gold Fort Christian which dates from the Dane's arrival in the 1660s. It now contains the Virgin Islands Museum tracing early and colonial life on St. Thomas. Beyond the old Grand Hotel and the neoclassical Post Office, at the head of Main Street, is the main shopping area. Here old brick and stone warehouse buildings bear well-known names alongside local stores. Other attractions on St. Thomas Island are the Government House, Estate St., Peter Greathouse and Coral World.

THE FRENCH ANTILLES

The French Antilles islands are dominated by the French. Martinique and Guadeloupe have tropical scenery and climate with a European lifestyle. Visitors can enjoy Guadeloupe's bustling capital Pointe-a-Pitre, its sandy beaches and rainforests. Martinique has historic towns and villages and the restaurants of Saint Martin and beach resorts of Saint Bathelemy. The tiny isles of Les Saintes, La Desirade and Marie-Galante offer white sand beaches and quiet island life. Variety and beauty are highlights of the French West Indies, made up of the single island of Martinique and the six islands which comprise the region of Guadeloupe.

The French Antilles have capitalized on their greatest assets because of the mingling of races from many lands and its enchanting environment. Tourism is important. The island people of Martinique and Guadeloupe are known for their natural beauty and Gallic style. French is the official language and French influence permeates island life. There are rain forests, sugar cane and tropical fruit. The people speak a form of Creole heard everywhere.

With a robust culture, fertile soil, abundant seas and a climate with high rainfall and many tourist attractions, The French Antilles have developed a happy balance of nature and lifestyle. Guadeloupe has two distinct halves. In the west is Basse-Terre, a rain forested volcanic area similar to Dominica. The Eastern wing is across the narrow Riviere-Salee (Salt River) called Grande-Terre which is a relatively flat, coral-based outcrop from a much older range of volcanoes.

Many of Guadeloupe's hotels are located along the southern shore of Grande-Terre, which offer watersports and interesting waterfront restaurants and bistros. Shattered limestone outcrop with rarest hills known as montagnes russes. Low plains reach out to the white, sandy beaches and spectacular, rocky cliffs along its coastline. The terrain on Basse-Terre is for the most part mountainous, rain forested and nourished by cascading waterfalls and mountain streams such as the Grande Riviere Goyaves which is the island's longest river at 20 miles. There are excellent golden sand beaches in the northwest.

Guadeloupe's climate is pleasant because of the trade winds. About 448,712 people live in the archipelago of Guadeloupe. Approximately 50 percent of the people are under 20 years of age. Most of them are of African descent. Some are descendants of early settlers, Bekes or of East Indian workers. Tourism and administration provide work for nearly half the population. Agriculture and industry are the other economic mainstays. The main language in Guadeloupe is French. Creole is the language of the people.

Pointe-A-Pitre is a large city along the coatline in Guadeloupe, with about 170,000 people. The Place de la Victoire is a large square with royal palms, mango trees, statues of famous Guadeloupeans and lined with cafes overlooking the busy harbor. La Dorse has ferries which depart for the offshore islands. The tourist information office is near La Darse. The cathedral is mainly metal to withstand occasional Caribbean hurricanes.

Crowded streets stretch in all directions overlooked by houses with interesting balconies and shutters. There is a main shopping district with a large marketplace with many kinds of produces. The Musee Schoelcher displays memorabilia associated with Victor Schoelcher, the 19th century anti-slavery campaigner. Musee St. John Perse traces the life of Alexis Saint-Leger, the Nobel Prize-winning Guadeloupean poet. The Aquarium de la Guadeloupe displays tropical fish. Fort Fleur d'Epee is an 18th century defensive bastion built of coral rock that has been partly restored.

Tourism centers are around the towns along Grande-Terre's south coast---Le Gosier, Ste Anne and St Francis---where beaches and waterfront restaurants are packed. North of this coastal area the country opens out and sugar cane fields rustle in the breeze. The quickest road to the capital town called Basse-Terre runs south along the island's eastern shore.

At the plantation Grand Café you can see a working banana plantation. Past Ste-Marie the route runs through the Allee du Manior, an avenue of 100 ft. royal palm trees. Near the coast there are Arawak carvings at the Parc Archeologigue des Roches Gravees dating from around AD 1000.

Other attractions are the Domaine de Severin at Ste-Rose and the story of sugar production is told at the Musee de Thum. Near the 17th century town of Pointe-Noire is the Maison du Bois, which shows local building techniques. Look at the Maison du Cacao to see a pictorial history of cocoa and chocolate. La Traversee crosses through the middle of Basse-Terre passing the Cascade aux Ecrivissea and the Maison de lat Foret which traces the development of the island's natural life.

Marie -Galante is the largest of Guadeloupe's offshore islands. It measures nearly 6 square miles and has a population of 12,400. Many of these people live in Grand-Bourg. The Chateau Muraet is a restored 18th century plantation house east of Grand-Bourg which contains a museum. There are walking paths around this island.

Les Saintes includes a nudist beach, scuba diving and a beautiful bay which is called a mini Rio. Terre-de-Bas and Terre-de-Haut are two inhabited places. There are beautiful beaches on Terre-de-Haut. Fort Napoleon has a museum and exotic garden.

SIGNIFICANT MOMENTS

There are other Caribbean islands such as Martinique, Saint-Barthelemy, Saint-Martin, Aruba, Bonaire, Curacao, Saba, Saint Eustatius and Saint Maarten. These Caribbean islands have magnificent beaches, interesting museums and sugar plantations. There are restaurants and bars close to the beaches. Tourists go swimming, scuba diving, surfing, snorkeling and boating.

JAMAICA

Jamaica is the third largest island in the Caribbean. This English speaking island enjoys all the character and vibrancy that has come to characterize the Caribbean. Some interesting places in Jamaica are Black River, Treasure Beach, Bamboo Avenue, Y.S. Falls, the Blue Mountains, Appleton Rum Estate in Cockpit Country and the National Gallery of Art in Kingston. Other attractions are National Heroes Park, Devon House, Bob Marly Museum and the Hope Botanical Gardens.

In Port Royal you can go to the Port Royal Museum and the Maritime Museum. The central town of Mandeville is known for Marshall's Pen and Pickapeppa Factory. Montego Bay has Sam Sharpe Square, Craft Market, Park Pit, Montego Bay Marine Park, Rose Hall, Greenwood Great House, Good Hope, Jamaica Rafting Rockland Feeding Station and Croydon in the Mountains.

Long Bay has one of the best beaches of 5 miles of superb sand with hotels and beach bars. Bloody Bar is where whalers cleaned their catch here. A lighthouse is at the southern end of Negril which has good views of the surrounding area. Ocho Rios is known for River Falls, St. Ann's Bay, Coyaba River Gardens, The Shaw Park Botanical Gardens, Fern Gully, Prospect Plantation, Harmony Hall, Irie Beach and Firefly.

Port Antonio is a charming town and east of town is Boston Bay and Reach Falls. Moore Town is an old maroon settlement.

THE CAYMAN ISLANDS

Many visitors fly to the Cayman Islands. Grand Cayman is the largest and most developed of the Caymans. You can visit the Islands National Museum, Cayman Turtle Farm, Stingray City, Pedro St. James Historic Site and Queen Elizabeth Botanic Park. Little Cayman and Cayman Brac are two other Cayman Islands.

CUBA

Cuba is strikingly different than the other Caribbean islands. Havana is Cuba's capital, which is less than 100 miles from Florida's Key West. 90 percent of visitors are from the U.S.A. However, US citizens are forbidden to spend their dollars in Cuba.

Cuba lies near the Gulf of Mexico and is the largest, Caribbean island. Much of the fertile land is covered with sugar cane. There are three mountain ranges in the west, the formation of the Sierra de los Organos, whose red earth is covered with tobacco plants, the Sierra Escambray, halfway along the island and Sierra Maestra in the island's eastern province, which includes the highest peak of Pico Turquino at 6,580 feet.

Cuba was Christopher Columbus' second landfall in 1492. Spanish adventurers came to Cuba. New World treasures flooded into Spain from Havana which quickly became the richest city in the Caribbean. Places to go are Old Havana, Soroa Orchid Gardens, Pinar de Rio, Vinales, Cojimar, Varadero, Cueva de Ambrosio, Cienfuegos, Tomas Theater, and Trinidad. Santiago de Cuba is the second town. You can see the cathedral Santa Iglesia Basilicia Metropolitana and El Uvero, a high point, and go to Pico Turquino, the highest peak in the Sierra Maestro at almost 6,000 feet.

HAITI

Haiti has excellent beaches and sophisticated hotels. Haiti is not recommended as a tourist destination at the present time. Haiti has an amazingly vibrant artistic and religious life. Its primitive-style art, with primary colors and cartoon-like forms, has been copied all over the Caribbean.

Voodoo is a mixture of Catholic and African beliefs described as "black magic" which runs deep in the Haitian psyche. Haiti has its own dance rhythm especially at Carnival time known as Mardi Gras.

PUERTO RICO

Puerto Rico is an important island in the Caribbean. San Juan is the best preserved Spanish colonial city in the Caribbean. Puerto Rico is an American territory. Many Americans visit this colorful, tropical island. This island offers endless exploration of rain forests, caves, mountains and hidden beaches. A coastal highway is the main road around the island of Puerto Rico.

Puerto Rico lies 994 miles southeast of Miami, Florida. It is 110 miles in length and about 37 miles from north to south with a range of mountains through the center of the island from east to west. On the north side there is rain forest and the rain in the northwest has created amazing karet cave systems. In the south the land is mainly dry and cactus-covered.

Both English and Spanish are mainly spoken in Puerto Rico. 3.9 million Puerto Ricans constitute a racial mix and include Africans, Spaniards, Italians and Lebanese. They are primarily Catholic. Their most important festivals are Saints' Days celebrations, combine a devout faith with the desire to dance, particularly to the salsa, a racing beat led by brass and African drums. The fiestas have costume balls, parades, picnics and fairs. The best known festival is the Festival of the Innocents on the 28th of December, in which the whole town of Hatillo on the north coast becomes a costume festivity. Music festivals are held throughout the year featuring different styles of island music.

Puerto Rico has traditional dishes with rice, plantains, crab, codfish batter balls or picadillas (meat or cheese-filled sandwiches. The most popular island pastimes are baseball and cockfighting.

The Cordillera Central is the major mountain range in Puerto Rico's interior, runs parallel to the coast, east and west on either side of the island's highest peak, Cerro de Punta. You can visit the ruta panoramica, Carite Forest Reserve, San Cristobal Canyon, Hacienda Gripinas, Caguana Indian Ceremonial Park, Arecibo Observatory, Cave Park, Mayaguez Zoo, Agricultural Research Station, Parque de Bombas, The Ponce Museum of Art,

Castillo Seralles, Tibes Indian Ceremonial Center and Hacienda Buena Vista.

The main road from Ponce to Mayaguez cuts inland and passes the town of San German with a seaside atmosphere with local seafood restaurants, cabins on stilts and small villas overlooking the mangroves on the coast. There is a nearby phosphorescent lake.

The new city of San Juan is historic. You can enjoy the colonial city, El Capitolio, the seat of Puerto Rican Senate and House of Representatives. Condado is a coastal, tourist town. You can visit the Isla Verde, the Rio Piedras Botanical Gardens and the Bacardi Rum Distillery and Museum.

Vieques and Culebra is sprinkled with islands and cays. A 45 minute ferry ride from the mainland brings you to Vieques where 8,000 inhabitants live. The central square is pleasant and has an information office. Esperanza is on the southern coast. Bars and restaurants are visible along the shorefront.

Culebra is a tranquil island site among a small crowd of tiny, coral outcrops, 25 miles east of the mainland. Only 1,600 islanders live on Culebra many in the only town of Dewey, also known as Pueblo. El Yunque Caribbean National Forest is a very impressive place. You can enjoy El Portal Rain Forest Center and the nature reserve at Las Cabezas de San Juan.

BARBADOS

Barbados is the most British of the Caribbean islands with safe and attractive beaches. It is prosperous, relaxed and welcoming. The east coast is quiet and undeveloped. Popular attractions include the famous rum; its lively south coast nightlife and passion for cricket.

Barbados has high-rise hotels, guesthouses and flats of the south. You can see underwater views from the dry comfort of the Atlantis Submarine. There are mahogany woodland, cattle and black bellied sheep grazing on meadows. There are traditional wooden chattel houses and forests of sugar cane.

You can enjoy the National Trust walk. Bridgetown is the capital of Barbados with old colonial buildings as well as modern offices. Bridgetown is the center of island life. You can visit Tyrol Cot Heritage Village and the Barbados Museum.

In Central Barbados you can visit the Francia Plantation, Sunbury Plantation House, Codrington College and St. John's Parish Church. Scotland is a hilly district in northeast Barbados, which is a series of peaks including Mount Hillaby. You can visit the Flower Forest, Turner's Hall Woods, Morgan Lewis Mill, the Grenade Hall Signal Station and Barbados Wildlife Reserve. On the South Coast you can see St. Lawrence Gap and Heritage Park and Four Square Rum Distillery.

The Caribbean islands are very picturesque with scenic, pristine beaches, rainforests, hidden coves and places to swim, snorkel, surf, go sailing and walking. You can learn about the Caribbean people and their culture.

THIRTY-TWO
WHY PEOPLE WORK

Why do people work? Well, many people work in order to make a living. People's bills must be paid such as rent, house payments, food, utilities, transportation, insurance, medical bills and other items. People who work usually get paid a monthly income or salary. The money they receive is used to buy what they need and want on a regular basis.

Sharon Weeden went to work in a glass factory. She worked from 7 a.m. until 4 p.m. Monday through Friday. She was paid every two weeks by her employer. Sharon worked in Chico, California. She commuted to work from Paradise which was twenty-five miles away. She went in a car pool in order to save money on gasoline.

The glass factory was hot during the day because burning furnaces were on all day. The furnaces were used to melt glass to be used to make glass objects, vases, pitchers, glasses and other shapes.

Sharon wore a protective mask over her face and gloves so she could avoid being burned by the hot furnaces and glass blowing equipment. She learned to use glass blowing equipment to shape melted glass into various shapes. She selected a variety of colored melted glass to work with. She was able to make a glass object every half hour. In one day Sharon created sixteen objects.

Each created object was blown into the specified shape. Then each object gradually hardened and cooled off. Once the shapes were dry and hardened, designs could be painted on each object. The final, completed pitchers, vases, glasses and other objects were displayed in a gallery room nearby the factory. Prices were written on toys near each glass object. Visitors who came to the glass factory were allowed to watch how glass is blown into objects. The visitors went to the display room to look at finished glass objects. Some visitors bought different, glass objects.

Sharon would sweat at work because the factory room rose to 110 degrees to 120 degrees with the burning furnaces on. She took a morning and afternoon coffee break in order to relax. She also had a 45 minute lunch break. Sharon ate her packed lunch in the employee lounge room.

Employees had staggered lunch breaks and different coffee break shifts because there were at least 50 employees. Sharon had been working at the glass factory for fourteen years and six months. She had learned how to create many glass objects.

Sharon started working at the glass factory when she was eighteen years old. She was nearly thirty-three years old. Sharon met another employee at the glassblowing factory. She had dated Kent for two years before they were married. They became acquainted during coffee breaks and lunch time.

Kent created glass objects at the glass factory. He had worked at this factory for sixteen years. Kent and Sharon worked in the same factory room. Both Kent and Sharon worked the same hours. They both received a paycheck every two weeks. It was necessary for both of them to work in order to pay their monthly bills.

THIRTY-THREE
WONDERLAND FANTASIES

Wonderland is a magnificent place to go to live in a blissful state of awareness. In THE WIZARD OF OZ, Dorothy traveled down a yellow brick road through an Emerald Kingdom. She encountered a straw man, Cowardly Lion and Tin man who traveled with her through the Land of Oz. This magical, enchanting wonderland came alive with talking flowers and trees. Dorothy finally came to the palace where the Oz lived. Dorothy was frightened by the Oz who hid behind a wall. The Oz spoke loudly with a very stern tone. He told Dorothy he couldn't help her to fulfill her wishes. He told her to leave the palace.

Dorothy discovered that the Oz was only an old man hiding behind a wall to avoid being known. She left the palace feeling disappointed in the Great Oz. She was told by her fairy queen to tap her magic red shoes three times and she would go home to Kansas. So, Dorothy tapped her red shoes three times. Sure enough, she was home in her own bed in Kansas. Dorothy recalled that people in her life in Kansas appeared to look like the people in her dream in the Land of Oz.

Alice went to Wonderland when she fell down a rabbit hole near a tree. She came to wonderland which was colorful, magical and enchanting. Alice came to a place where there was a tea party with the Mad Hatter. He encountered a Cheshire cat in a tree smiling at her. She sat at the tea table to visit with the Mad Hatter. Then she went to see the Queen of Spades.

Alice saw the Queen of Spades' palace. It was an enchanting place. Alice saw soldiers dressed in colorful uniforms and big soldiers' hats. Men and women were dressed in traditional costumes of the 17th century. There were trees and flowers everywhere. Wonderland was a land of cartoon figures.

Alice finally escapes from Wonderland when she wakes up under a big tree. She realized that she was dreaming about Wonderland, which seemed to be so real.

We can dream about a wonderland of our own. In a dream we create unusual places and have enchanting experiences. A dreamer may see sparkling diamond light and magnificent colors swirling around. Stars may glitter and sunsets may blaze over a beautiful ocean.

Beautiful, graceful beings may move about chanting celestial melodies and singing heavenly songs. They may be dressed in white, gold and purple robes with sparkling sandals. These spiritual beings move about promoting peace, harmony and loving feelings. They express goodwill and a blissful co-existence.

Each wonderland may be magical and enchanting with a variety of magnificent settings and unusual experiences. You can make a fantasy seem real in another dimension and dream. It is really happening in that dimensional dream.

THIRTY-FOUR
IS TELEVISION HEALTHY TO WATCH?

There are many television programs. Television programs are TCM, IFC, WE, C-SPAN, TNT, Fox News, Comedy Central, National Geographic, Hallmark, The Learning Channel, History Channel, Lifetime Movies, Science, Biography, Discovery, Home, A & E, Animal Planet, Starz, Encore Action, Encore Drama, Fox Movie, HBO West, HBO East, HBO Comedy, More Max, Travel Channel, Local News Channel and many more channels.

Some television channels such as the Travel Channel present places around the world with worthwhile narrations from travel hosts such as Samantha Brown, Anthony Bourdain and Ian Wright. Much can be learned from travelogues seen on television. Travelogues are about specific places which includes cities, cultural highlights, natural resources, recreational activities and picturesque scenery. You can learn about foods, art, artifacts, history, political and social leaders. Travelogues can awaken us to what different locations look like and how people live, speak, eat and enjoy life.

Some Turner Classic Movies (TCM) are worth seeing on television. Movies made in the 1920s, 1930s, 1940s, 1950s, 1960s and on generally show what people believe in and how they lived in different generations. C-Span and Fox News, CNN and local news programs update us on what is happening in the world. We can find out what people are doing and how they behave.

National Geographic television programs are educational because landscapes, oceans, rivers, jungles, swamps, meadows, safari land, mountains and valleys are shown and described. We can learn about wild life, ocean life and the plant kingdom as well as about minerals, gems and rocks. We can learn a lot about our Earth when we watch National Geographic programs.

Hallmark is a family television program. Prairie and western lifestyles are presented such as THE LITTLE HOUSE ON THE PRAIRIE, WAGON TRAIN and other Western Dramas. We are able to develop an understanding of the Old West and what it was like to settle in prairie country. Lifestyles two hundred years ago are described and dramatized so we can identify with the way people lived two hundred years ago.

Science programs on television are educational because scientists present specific knowledge and information about our Universe, about our solar system and our Earth. New concepts are presented to show how scientists discover new information while they use the scientific method.

Starz, HBO and Encore Drama usually present human interest dramas and action flicks which describe lessons to be learned. Some human action plots and stories are worthwhile. When dramas are realistic they may help us learn lessons and we can evaluate human behavior.

Biographies about well known people and leaders help us appreciate how, why, where and when important people lived and contributed their leadership, important influences, service and goodwill to make worthwhile changes in the world. Great writers, politicians, teachers, artists, philosophers, doctors and public leaders have made a difference because of their achievements and use of their abilities and talents.

There are television programs which are not healthy and can be harmful for children and even adults to watch. Murder dramas, sexual exposures, unclean movies with violence and vulgarity are detrimental to mental and emotional well being. People who watch television constantly should avoid negative television programs which are emotionally and mentally draining and upsetting to watch.

There is a time and place to watch well selected television programs. I have described healthy programs to watch. There are a number of quality music channels to listen to relaxing and harmonious music as well. Select television channels which provide educational and worthwhile programs. Avoid television programs that pull you down. What you view on television affects your health and well being. So, select wisely what you watch on television.

THIRTY-FIVE
OUR FAVORITE FOODS

We all have favorite foods that we like to eat. Food which tastes delicious is desirable to eat. Nutritious food such as apples, bananas, oranges, grapes, grapefruit, pears and mangos are delicious. Raw vegetables such as tomatoes, parsley, carrots, green and red peppers and cabbage are nutritious as well as delicious.

Many people like to eat "junk" foods such as twinkies, hot dogs, candy, cake and cookies made with white flour and sugar, potato chips and corn chips. Greasy foods and food loaded with sugar and chemicals are harmful to eat. People enjoy the taste of "junk" foods unfortunately. Many children want to eat rich, sugary foods. Desserts are their favorite foods. They eat ice cream, cakes, puddings, cookies, chips, and drink colas and punch.

Unfortunately, foods that may taste delicious may not be good for us. We should be careful what we eat. Eating too much and eating too quickly can be harmful. Food must be digested carefully. The right combination of foods should be assimilated to maintain good health.

Baked and grilled meat and fish can be prepared well to taste delicious. Potatoes can be baked. Potato skins are good to eat. Many vitamins are in potato skins which are valuable and nutritious.

Nutritious salads such as mixed fruit can be sliced and blended which tastes good. Fruit salads make good snacks. Oatmeal cookies made with borwn sugar and natural oats and raisins taste very good. The fiber in oatmeal cookies is beneficial to promote good health.

THIRTY-SIX
ENDLESS POSSIBILITIES

Endless possibilities exist in our lives. We have the opportunity to develop our abilities and talents. Our interests, hobbies and specific activities are experiences which can help us to fulfill our lives. We can learn to play musical instruments, sing solos, write poetry, paint pictures and present speeches in public.

Many children learn to play various games such as baseball, basketball, football, tennis, volleyball and other sports. Some of these children grow up to become professional baseball players, professional basketball players, professional football players, professional tennis and other sports.

When we make an effort to develop our potentials such as our abilities and talents we are more personally fulfilled because we are developing awareness by being creative and helpful to others. The ability to entertain others by performing for many audiences as a musician is rewarding. The ability to write descriptive and interesting poems is a worthwhile endeavor.

Creative individuals are able to inspire and encourage others to be creative. Seamstresses are able to design and sew different clothes which are interesting to wear and to look at. An artist is capable of painting beautiful ocean scenes, sunsets, different landscapes, still life scenes, flowers and even portraits. An artist can learn how to paint a variety of scenes.

If we make an effort to develop our potentials we have an opportunity to develop a variety of skills and talents. We have many chances to change our lives so we can improve our lives. We just need to try and to make an effort to develop our abilities and potentials.

THIRTY-SEVEN
NEGATIVE AND POSITIVE
SITUATIONS

People encounter negative and positive situations in their lives. Negative situations can occur which disrupt our lives. How can we handle negative situations in order to solve difficulties which may suddenly take place? We need to keep as calm and collected as possible. We need to think of solutions as quickly as possible to remedy and overcome the negative situations.

Examples of negative situations are when someone accuses you of something you didn't do. This person wants to blame you for something that didn't happen or that someone else may have done. This person continues to accuse you for taking something out of his house without permission. He thinks you robbed him of some household silverware and gold goblets.

You are faced with proving that you didn't steal the silverware and gold goblets. Your accuser only knows you, Clint Woodward, have been in his house visiting for a period of time. He didn't witness who may have taken these household items. So, you have to find a way to convince him that you weren't the one who stole these valuable items.

So, you decide to talk to your accuser calmly. You say, "Has anyone else come over to see you recently?" Your accuser,

Joe Heley, looks at you with a frown. He then states, "I have friends who come over. They wouldn't steal from me!" You reply, "Anyone of them may have stolen your silverware and goblets. Check for fingerprints where these household items were placed."

Joe Heley looked at Clint with a doubtful expression. Joe answered, "Why would my friends steal from me?" Clint replied, "You are trusting all of your friends. Yet, maybe one or two of your friends may have taken these items. I certainly did not steal them!"

Clint maintained his self control. Joe looked upset. He didn't want to accuse any of his friends. Joe walked over to the place where the silverware and gold goblets once existed in his house. He checked for fingerprints. He wasn't able to trace any fingerprints. Joe spoke to Clint with agitation, "I can't see any fingerprints! How will I know who stole from my house? You claim you didn't do it!"

Clint looked at Joe with understanding. He knew Joe was upset. Clint did not become angry or out of control. Instead, he said, "I am sorry anyone would steal from you".

Clint looked at Joe with understanding. He knew Joe was upset. Clint did not become angry or out of control. Instead, he said, "I am sorry anyone would steal from you. I suggest you call everyone who has been to your house recently. Maybe your friends saw who took your household items." Joe looked at Clint and appeared less accusingly at Clint. He replied, "I feel uncomfortable about questioning my friends." Clint responded, "If you want to resolve this situation you need to investigate carefully. I will ask around, too."

Clint decided to leave Joe's house. He went home. He thought about Joe's situation. Clint decided to call the people who had come over to see Joe recently. He asked each of them about the silverware and gold goblets. No one that he called mentioned that they saw who took these things.

The next day Clint went over to see Joe. He told him that he had investigated about these household items that had disappeared. Joe knew Clint was concerned about what happened. Joe apologized to Clint about accusing him of stealing these items. Clint replied, "Thanks for accepting that I did not steal them."

Joe continued to investigate who might have stolen his valuable, household items. Clint continued to develop a friendship with Joe. Joe realized that Clint cared what happened to him. As a result Joe respected Clint for maintaining his self control during a trying time. Clint was able to take a negative situation and turn it into a neutral situation because he maintained a much calmer approach to this negative situation.

Diane McGee was a cheerful, optimistic person. She was a positive person, who served and helped her family, friends and acquaintances. Diane attended church almost every Sunday. She greeted her church friends and members as well as the minister cheerfully and warmly.

Diane served in church committees and she participated in the church choir every Sunday. She attended choir rehearsals to prepare for Sunday choir presentations. She had become the choir director after another choir director had resigned. Diane was positive in her approach as a choir director. She encouraged the sopranos, altos, tenors and bass members to sing in rhythm, in tune and with self confidence.

The church choir performed well every Sunday. The church members in the audience praised Diane McGee and the choir because they enjoyed the choir music.

Members of the church befriended Diane because she was so likeable. Diane's friends spoke highly about her because Diane was kind, supportive and loving towards her friends. Diane was popular and respected because of her positive approach to life. Her positive attitude made a difference to others. She was a well adjusted, happy person who achieved her goals.

THIRTY-EIGHT
GLOBAL WARMING

Global warming has become a world problem. Many people are concerned about the Earth warming more and more. The North Pole glaciers are melting which is causing more water to rise. This can eventually cause flooding of Canada and North America.

Global warming has been occurring for a period of time. As snow and ice melts the continents will change and possibly shift. Shiftng of land can cause earthquakes and changing weather conditions.

As the weather continues to become warmer the sun will be hotter causing the earth to become scorched. Polar bears are affected by the warmer climate at the North Pole. Polar bears are decreasing in numbers because of the climate changes.

If more glaciers continue to melt in the North Pole region eventually Canada, Alaska and North America (the U.S.A.) will probably sink under a rising ocean. Other continents will be affected by the rising ocean which may totally flood the Northern Hemisphere. Europe may also sink under the rising ocean.

Global warming is caused by manmade pollution caused from chemicals, sprays, carburetor exhaust and manmade smoke. Air pollution should be prevented. We need to make a global effort to clean up the Earth's air. We need to cleanse our oceans, lakes, streams and creeks in order to have cleaner water to drink and to cook our food. We need to cleanse the soil on Earth.

Global warming might be controlled if humanity would take care of the Earth. Everyone should make an effort to protect our planet Earth.

THIRTY-NINE
DEPENDENCE AND INDEPENDENCE

Many people are dependent on others because they are handicapped, elderly or sick. It is important to be able to rely on others when we need help. Dependent people need assistance and special care. Dependent people count on others to take care of their needs.

Children from the age of birth to the age of 18 live with their parents to look after them. Children need guidance and personal care. Small infants need much more personal care and attention. As children continue to grow year by year they become more and more independent. They learn step by step to take care of themselves.

For example children learn to dress themselves. They learn to tie their shoe strings. Then children learn to put on shirts, blouses, pants and dresses. They learn to comb their hair and cut their fingernails. Parents teach their children to make them beds, to sweep, mop and to vacuum and dust their home.

Eventually children become more independent as they become teenagers. By then, they have learned all their personal grooming, household chores and they may have learned to cook as well as how to drive a car. In time young adults must work outside their homes and hold jobs.

SIGNIFICANT MOMENTS

The more independent a person becomes the more he or she is able to experience freedom and inner strength. Independent individuals are able to experience many things. Independence brings fulfillment and self achievement. So, we should learn to become more independent day by day, month by month and year by year to achieve many goals.

FORTY
REVOLVING OBJECTS

Revolving objects capture our attention. Revolving doors exist in hotels and large buildings. The Top of the Mar revolves around so people can view the city of San Francisco. The Space Needle in Seattle, Washington revolves around. People witness a magnificent view of Seattle.

Revolving objects may be maintained because of mechanical devices and methods. The Earth revolves around the Sun. All our planets revolve around the Sun. Planetoids and moons also revolve around planets. Revolving objects spiral around such as moving mobiles. Balls on strings may revolve around in circles. Revolving objects are affected by gravitational pull. Satellites in space revolve around our planet, Earth. These satellites may be used to take pictures of the Earth. Satellites may be used to study the Earth and other planets in our solar system. Our atmosphere and temperatures on Earth may be measured and observed by moving cameras.

Thousands of revolving objects such as asteroids float and move between Mars and Jupiter. They continue to revolve. However, some asteroids pull away from their regular revolving orbits. They may be moving towards our Earth.

SIGNIFICANT MOMENTS

Scientists are trying to find effective ways to stop large destructive asteroids from coming to our planet. Large asteroids can destroy the surface of the Earth because they cause dust debris. 65 million years ago scientists believe a large asteroid caused dinosaurs to become extinct. Earthquakes caused the Earth to open up. Dinosaurs fell into large cracks and died. As a result, many creatures and plants died because of lack of water, air and food. It took time for life to be restored on the Earth's surface.

Revolving planets exist in other solar systems. The Universe also revolves around in its existing orbit and time dimension. Revolving objects may always exist in the Cosmos.

FORTY-ONE
HIRING AND FIRING EMPLOYEES

Employers interview new, possible employees. They ask applicants questions about their previous job experiences and educational background. They go over applicants' resumes and letters of recommendations.

Once a person is selected for employment he or she has been hired by an employer. The new employee is shown what job responsibilities and duties to perform day by day. The employee is expected to perform expected duties using his or her skills. The employer expects all employees to complete all tasks and responsibilities they are assigned to complete.

If any employee is constantly late to work without good reason this employee may in time lose his or her job. An employee who slacks off and doesn't finish his or her work may be fired by the employer. The employer may give several warnings first about the employee's inefficiency and incomplete work. If an employer notices that work assignments are not correctly done, this may be another reason to fire an employee.

Employers maintain certain expectations and standards. Goals and objectives are developed. Some employers give many chances if they especially like an employee. However, the employee must improve on the job. He or she can be fired if he or she doesn't improve in time.

Employers usually don't like to fire employees. Yet, if the work isn't done correctly, or isn't finished, employers will lose business and money. So, employers are capable of hiring and firing employees when they are having problems with certain employees.

FORTY-TWO
FIDDLE A DEE!

Fiddle A Dee is often an expression meaning oh well-come see come saw! People may take experiences challanty and respond with a carefree attitude. It helps to have a detached attitude in order to maintain a neutral response when something startling happens.

Peter Shelling was walking down a main street one day in a town, Bethany, where he grew up in. He knew many people who lived in this town. Peter usually participated in town events and activities. He was helpful and usually expressed concern and interest when something unusual occurred.

While Peter continued down the busy street he noticed many people and shops. He kept to himself. He noticed colorful shops as he approached an art gallery down this street. Before he reached the art gallery he encountered a commotion in the street. Several men were fighting in the street. They appeared angry at a certain man dressed in a black shirt and blue jeans who wore a large, black cowboy hat and black boots.

This man was approximately 6 foot seven inches tall. He appeared to be very strong. He shoved the other man away from him when they attempted to create violent blows. They fell on the hard pavement when he threw them aside to the ground.

Finally, the three men gave up because they were injured while they lay on the pavement in the street.

Meanwhile, Peter, who had been watching this violent spectacle, continued to stand there. He was amazed at the tall man's strength and ability to defend himself. Peter thought quietly, "I'm glad I didn't get involved in this street brawl. He thought to himself, "Fiddle A Dee." It is best not to get involved in such a violent confrontation. Peter finally walked away relieved to be safe and not injured.

FORTY-THREE
PHYSICAL THERAPY

P hysical therapy treatments are available in most larger towns and cities. Physical therapists have been trained to massage people who have physical ailments. Physical therapy treatments can help heal people with physical handicaps.

Physical therapists usually provide a special therapy bed and they may use electrical equipment and massage techniques. People who have special physical handicaps need regular treatments and certain muscles and bones may need gradual adjustments.

Physical therapists are able to release tension and aches in certain places in the body. Oils and penetrating creams may be used and applied to the skin. These oils and creams help to loosen up muscles.

People who have been in serious accidents need a lot of help to recover from physical injuries and ailments. Daily, the therapeutic exercises should be experiences in order to gradually heal from accidents. Physical therapists should be patient and apply careful therapeutic methods with each patient. In time different patients may be healed because of physical therapy treatments.

SIGNIFICANT MOMENTS

Different exercises such as stretching, bending, raising arms and legs, jumping and hopping movements help to limber the body. Pulling up and pushing are other techniques. Push-ups and crossing arms and legs help to strengthen arm and leg muscles.

It is wise to call a physical therapist for appointments. Special treatments with physical treatments can make a difference in recovering from physical injuries and ailments.

FORTY-FOUR
ALL ABOUT BOOKS

Books are very valuable. There are many types of books available. Books can be bought at bookstores, newsstands, shops and sales at public libraries. Also, books are sold at book fairs, at book signings and at schools.

Books provide knowledge and information about many subjects, topics and issues. Books can be purchased at used bookstores as well. Usually books are in certain sections in places like Wal-Marts, K-Marts, at larger, grocery stores and even at garage sales.

Books provide readers with valuable information about many memorable experiences. There are many types of books such as novels, nonfiction, biographies, reports, encyclopedia facts, travelogues, science digests, adventures, movie and television reviews and critiques and national geographic experiences.

Books enrich our lives with many ideas, opinions and feelings about people, places, events, things and personal experiences. So, enjoy browsing for books. Enjoy reading regularly to learn about many facts, ideas and beliefs.

FORTY-FIVE
WHY SOME PEOPLE ARE CALLED BUMS

W hy are some people labeled as bums? Bums are people who refuse to work to earn a living especially when they are very capable of working. Bums usually lay around in the street or alleys. They may beg for money and food.

Bums may be found dwelling on beaches and in parks. They usually carry a backpack on them. They may sleep on park benches, under trees, on the beach or anywhere else where they can lie down.

Bums depend on other people to feed them, clothe them and provide them with shelter. They avoid working at all costs. They prefer to be lazy and sit around doing nothing.

Don Haskins carried a backpack on his back. He wore an old shirt, ripped, old blue jeans, an old jacket and old boots. He wore a baseball hat to keep sunlight off his face. Don lingered in a public park during the day time. At night he put a bedroll on the grass under a big pine tree. He was used to sleeping outside at night.

Stars and the Moon came out at night. Don got into his bedroll and he looked up at the stars and Moon and he enjoyed locating constellations and star patterns. Don slept outside night after night because he was homeless. He didn't want to sleep in a shelter.

Don had been homeless for at least ten years because he didn't work to earn a living. He went to a church everyday to eat a free lunch. He usually ate an apple and any fruit he was given for breakfast. The free lunch was his best meal of the whole day.

Don often begged for loose change from people in the park and downtown in the streets. He received some small change occasionally. He used this money to buy food such as fruit and nuts as well as cold drinks. Don managed to survive on the food that he ate. He had to endure cold temperatures at night when he slept outside in the park.

Don continued day by day living like a bum. He refused to look for a job. He was able to stay alive because he had enough to eat and a place to sleep. He accepted his lifestyle. Don didn't think of himself as a bum.

FORTY-SIX
STILL LIFE COLLECTIONS

Still life collections are usually kept in some art galleries. Still life art is a drawing or painting which illustrates fruit in a bowl, or a vase with flowers, or objects on a table. Each still life scene illustrates stillness of objects which captivate the viewers and awareness of objects which are not moving.

The Gugenheim Museum displays many still life scenes. This art museum is in New York City. The Paul Getty Art Gallery displays a collection of still life scenes. The Paul Getty Art Gallery is in Los Angeles and New York City.

Still life art work has been known for many centuries. Flowers such as roses, daisies, lilies, poppies and many other flowers are drawn in vases. These still life scenes usually are very colorful and realistic looking. Rose can look very beautiful and the petals and center of roses can be drawn with descriptive details. Poppies such as orange, red and yellow colors look realistic even in still life scenes. Other flowers such as lilies and daffodils as well as sunflowers look very interesting even in still life scenes.

Still life scenes can vary depending on what objects are put together to sketch and to paint. Still life scenes will continue to be sketched in black and white and with paints. Large art galleries display still life scenes.

FORTY-SEVEN
SELECTING TEXTBOOKS

Selecting worthwhile textbooks to be used in classrooms is important to promote quality education.

A textbook should be selected based on its contents, illustrations, information and knowledge. The way the knowledge is put together, use of vocabulary and follow-up exercises and tests. A quality textbook should up-to-date information and the most recent knowledge.

Colorful and illustrated textbooks impress students more than textbooks without colorful illustrations and examples. Colorful photographs usually impress readers.

Each school should have a selection textbook committee. Textbook committees should carefully select effective textbooks. The committee for new textbooks should compare different textbooks so they can evaluate each textbook. By using specific criteria the committee can determine which textbooks are best to select.

Students learn more from textbooks that are well written. A well written textbook will be of much benefit to students. New textbooks should be selected every five years so up-to-date knowledge and information can be added to educate students.

FORTY-EIGHT
WHY PEOPLE ARE CREATIVE

Why are certain people creative while other people tend to be far less creative? Creative people are inquisitive, curious and enthusiastic about learning. Creative people want to express their talents and abilities.

Uncreative people tend to seek uncreative jobs where they are uncreative. Creative people usually select jobs which are interesting and more stimulating. Creative individuals develop specific abilities and talents such as becoming a musician, an artist, a writer, a photographer, an inventor and a scientist. Many more creative experiences can be achieved.

It is worthwhile to be a creative person. A creative person generally is happier and definitely more productive and industrious.

FORTY-NINE
EFFECTS FROM SOUNDS

Sounds effect life on Earth and even in outer space. The sound of the ocean waves and moving currents have a rhythmic sound which may be relaxing to listen to. The sound of wind also affects living things. Loud winds have a much stronger sound. So, loud winds are more noticeable.

The sounds of cars, buses, trains and airplanes all have certain mechanical sounds. Vehicles make loud sounds. We especially notice these sounds especially at night when we want to sleep quietly. Unnatural, harsh sounds which are manmade have harsh sounds which affect our state of mind.

Sounds of birds usually sound natural and melodic. Birds chirp and express high pitched sounds. Each bird has a different sound. Owls have a less melodic sound. Hoot owls make their calls usually at night. Geese produce honking sounds to alert other geese. Whippoorwills produce high pitched sounds which usually are melodic. Crows make cawing sounds which are sharp and demanding. Crows try to scare people away from their territory. Seagulls make harsh guttural sounds.

Cows make moo-moo sounds. Sheep make ba ba sounds. Goats make ba ba sounds as well. Each animal makes its own sound, which affects other creatures in nature. All life is in motion and gives out its own specific sounds and vibrations.

Humanity listens to different kinds of music on the radio, television and records. People like to sing and play musical instruments. We will always be affected by different sounds around us which come from various sources.

FIFTY
GETTING ALONG WITH RELATIVES

Getting along with relatives can be a challenging experience if they are unfriendly, disagreeable and uncaring. Some relatives may be friendly, open, kind and caring. It is important to have helpful, loving and caring parents especially during childhood days.

Cousins and nephews may be rambunctious and difficult to get along with. Some cousins and nephews may be pleasant, social and cooperative. If you make an effort to reach out to your relatives you will have a better chance to know them and to get along with them.

Your attitude and approach will usually make a difference if you want to have a positive relationship with your relatives. You can organize a family reunion and you can invite as many relatives to come so you can socialize with them. A positive approach will help you relate better with them.

Relatives can be nice as well as kind to you. Relatives, who remember your birthday and send you a card at Christmas and at Easter time, are thoughtful. Relatives that call you and who write to you are attentive and even more caring. Stay away from relatives who are consistently unfriendly and thoughtless. Certain relatives may become very worthwhile friends. You may be able to receive help and protection from certain relatives during a crisis. You may be able to reach out to them to take care of you. Some relatives may care about you almost as much as your parents cared about you. If you have been thoughtful, generous and kind to them they may extend a helping hand when you need help.

FIFTY-ONE
EXPECTATIONS

We all have certain expectations in our lives. We expect certain accomplishments to be achieved. For instance, in school many students want to pass examinations and earn good grades to receive praise and recognition from others. People who participate in certain sports want to win games to receive honors and recognition from many people who want them to win.

We are expected to live by man-made laws and rules. In school we are expected to obey our teachers and to complete our assignments. At home we are expected to obey our parents. We may be expected to do chores such as making our bed, putting our clothes away, dusting, mopping, vacuuming, washing dishes, weeding the garden, etc.

When we are hired to do a job we are expected to follow through with certain duties and responsibilities. We are expected to be on time and work eight hours usually. We are expected to complete each duty. We usually develop certain goals and objectives while we are working. Our employers expect us to do a good and efficient job. If anyone doesn't consistently perform expected duties that person may be dismissed and fired.

SIGNIFICANT MOMENTS

Expectations occur throughout our lifetimes. We are expected to learn to take care of ourselves. We are supposed to keep clean and change our clothes regularly. We are expected to come home after school unless we have after school activities. We are expected to be in bed on school nights at a reasonable time. We are expected to get up early enough so we can go to school or to a job.

Without expectations, goals and objectives a person would not be motivated to achieve any goals and few or no achievements. So, certain goals and objectives should be created and we should try to accomplish them. We will be more fulfilled if we fulfill our goals.

FIFTY-TWO
WHY DO WE THINK WE ARE LIMITED?

A person may feel limited by their upbringing, religious beliefs and school training. An individual has been influenced to believe that he or she is not able to accomplish by developing new awareness, creativity and by experimenting.

If a person is taught to avoid driving a car because he or she is told it is very dangerous, this person may not learn to drive a car. This person goes on a bus, train or walks to his destination. This person is limited because of the fear to drive.

If a woman is told that she is inferior to a man from early childhood on she grows up feeling she is inferior to men. As a result, this girl who becomes a woman, allows men to dominate her. She doesn't learn to be independent and she doesn't make important decisions for herself. She feels inadequate and insecure. She waits for her father, brothers and husband to make decisions for her.

Some individuals, who have done poorly in elementary school and high school, decide not to go to college. These individuals do not enroll in college. They accept menial jobs with no academic stimulation or challenge. These individuals feel very limited because they have not developed their abilities.

They have not become educated. They feel limited in what they are able to do.

Limitations are created by one's mind. A person, who becomes filled with fear, anxieties, stress and limitations, feels insecure and he or she does not use his or her imagination and creative potentials.

Children should be taught to develop their abilities and talents from an early age on. Children should be raised to overcome limitations so they can be fulfilled as they grow up. Individuals should have the opportunity to become educated and to become free thinkers so they can live worthwhile lives.

FIFTY-THREE
CRITERIONS FOR LIVING

Each person usually develops criterions for living. To create a peaceful, harmonious lifestyle is an important criterion. Each day should be lived to the fullest. We can learn a lot by observing nature. Our awareness of living creatures and plants helps us understand God's creations.

The laws of the Cosmic plan can be learned and lived by. The law of love, law of centralization, law of unity and harmony should be understood. We should realize that love should be the center of our lives. The law of karma, known as cause and effect, is an important law. We need to realize how cause and effect takes place in our lives.

Criterions for living are goals and standards we live by. Our goals and purposes for living are what we learn to live by. Our religious convictions are important for us to live by. When we live with an awareness of God as a divine creator and giver of life our lives have much more meaning.

Criterions help us have direction and purpose for our lives. We need to develop specific reasons for how we behave and relate to others. Our criterions are our guidelines.

FIFTY-FOUR
WILL HUMANITY SURVIVE?

Many people wonder if humanity will survive. The end of the Earth is a concern for many people. It is a question of cycles and time. The Earth operates within a Manavantara of 432,000,000 years.

Asteroids are moving between Mars and Jupiter. Some asteroids have moved out of orbit and may be heading toward the Earth. A large asteroid may reach Earth in several years. Scientists are trying to find ways to stop this asteroid from hitting the Earth.

If a large asteroid were to fall to Earth it would cause severe damage to the Earth's surface. The poles would be pulled out of alignment. Dust storms would block the sun from the Earth's atmosphere.

Humanity would be doomed if a large asteroid fell to Earth. We need fresh air and food to survive. We need a safe environment to live in. If thick dust is floating around it is difficult to breathe. People become unhealthy when they have to breathe unclean, polluted air. If food becomes scarce and unavailable, people die from starvation.

If scientists can find effective ways to stop asteroids from falling to Earth, humanity will be able to survive. Harmful, contagious diseases can cause millions of people to die. Vaccinations are given for contagious diseases. Some diseases are causing rapid deaths because no vaccinations are available to stop them such as AIDS and certain kinds of viruses.

The year 2012 is a year of deep concern for many people. The ancient Mayans predicted the end of a cycle or the end of the Earth. The Mayan calendar will end on December 21, 2012. Many people are worried about what will happen on this date.

Only God, our Divine Creator, knows what will happen on Earth. God has developed a divine plan for all living creatures. God's plan for humanity is divine. There are cycles and root races for humanity to experience. Presently, we are in the fourth and fifth root races. The sixth root race will evolve on Earth someday.

It is possible that America and Europe will sink under the ocean someday. People living on these continents will reincarnate on other continents to evolve in the future. Humanity has changed and evolved in many cycles.

Atomic bombs and dangerous weapons of destruction should be neutralized and not be used. The destructive methods of warfare should be banned from the world. The survival of humanity depends on protection of the Earth. We need to live in harmony and peace on Earth to survive.

FIFTY-FIVE
FLOATING ICEBERGS

Many large icebergs float around near the North Pole, South Pole and upper region near Iceland and Greenland as well as Alaska. Seals, walruses and Polar bears dwell on large icebergs.

Seals and walruses must be on guard when they lie down on icebergs to sun themselves and to rest. Polar bears are known to sneak up on seals and baby walruses unexpectedly to capture them to eat.

Walruses may swim for many miles in the ocean looking for a floating iceberg to climb on to rest and to sun themselves. Baby walruses are protected by their parents on icebergs. They follow their parents wherever they go.

Baby seals also follow their parents. They must learn to swim shortly after they are born. They must learn to climb onto icebergs where they dwell with their parents. Seals navigate under ice covered ocean water which is very cold. They stay in the ocean for some time. However, when they see open holes in the ice covered oceans they go up for air.

Polar bears create holes in the ice. Seals tend to be seen at the open holes. The polar bears catch an unsuspecting seal so it can eat it. Many times seals swim away from an open hole if they see a polar bear near the hole. The polar bear has to wait for another seal to appear at the open hole.

Floating icebergs eventually melt during warmer months of summer. Seals and walruses dwell on much smaller icebergs and they must move to any available icebergs.

When no more icebergs are available seals and walruses must find rocks in the ocean to dwell on. They also dwell on the open landscape in summertime. The sun shines for nearly 22 hours a day during summer months.

Floating icebergs are usually huge. These icebergs go down for many feet and remain solid for many months. Icebergs break away from the regular landscape. During winter months the snow and ice is very solid. As it warms up hundreds of icebergs begin to form and float away.

Birds also dwell on icebergs. Seabirds which can cope with colder climates may dwell on icebergs in the summer time as they migrate at Alaska, the Aleutian Islands and other small upper region islands and in the Antarctic region.

FIFTY-SIX
LOOK BEYOND THE HORIZON

Look beyond the sunrise beyond the horizon. You will see more beauty as you travel passed what you have seen. More and more horizons will appear before your eyes. God's creations continue to awaken your mind and heart force to the unknown beyond each horizon.

Every horizon is the final point at the edge of the Earth. Our imagination can soar wondering what we will see beyond each horizon. We may drive or sail to that unknown place where our vision wants to take us. We will continue to experience new horizons as we search for new dimensions in space and time.

Vivid memories awaken our minds and feelings to splendid colors, shapes and visions beyond compare. So, enjoy each horizon and experience fantastic views beyond the horizon.

FIFTY-SEVEN
REMOTE PLACES

Remote places may awaken you to unknown experiences. You may go to an unknown island in the Pacific or Atlantic Ocean. No one is living there or few people dwell there. Deserts are remote places. Jungles can be remote if you travel to an isolated, unknown location.

Sally and Homer Applestead were explorers. They enjoyed traveling to unusual, remote places. The Applesteads decided to travel to a remote area in upper Alaska by boat to unknown land where no one else had ever ventured to travel. They packed camping equipment such as a tent, wooden stakes, a hammer to pitch the wooden stakes in the ground, cooking utensils and metal plates, silverware, cups and canned and dried goods.

Homer and Sally decided to draw a map to describe the unknown landscape. They wanted to explore the wilderness to find new places to appreciate. They lived in Nome, Alaska on the Central Western Coast near the Bering Sea.

Homer and Sally decided to travel in a small plane across the northern region of Alaska. They packed their supplies in the small plane which they rented to go exploring in Alaska. Homer piloted the plane. Sally and he left the Nome Airport in the small plane. Homer flew over Pilgrim Springs, Igloo over the Seward Peninsula to Taylor. Homer continued over Deering. He traveled over the Chukchi Sea past Kotzebue to Noatak on the coast and over the Misheguk Mountains and Tingmerpuk Mountains.

As Homer and Sally traveled over the Misheguk Mountains they saw thick, blue ice in glacier formations. When they continued over Tengmerkpuk Mountains there was more blue snow covered on these mountains plus glaciers. The temperature had become much colder. It was 30 degrees below zero in the sky. It began to snow and snow was covered on the small plane. The moving blades produced energy in the airplane motors. If these blades became stuck with ice and solid snow the airplane would not operate properly.

Homer decided to raise the small airplane above the snow clouds to avoid more snow. He hoped the ice would melt near the moving motor blades. Homer continued towards Colville. He decided to land in a field near this town. He brought the plane down gradually to the field.

The field near Colville was covered with ice and some melting snow. It was summertime in Alaska. The sun remained visible for three-fourths of the long day. Homer and Sally were glad to be on the ground. They decided to camp out near Colville to allow their rented plane to be checked for safety. They needed to fill the gas tank before continuing on their journey.

Homer and Sally set up their tent in the wet field. Some wild flowers were growing in this field. Melted snow provided water to help the wild flowers and grass to grow. Once the tent was carefully pitched Homer began building a fire so Sally could warm up some food for them to eat. Homer placed cut wood in a hole he had dug. He placed folded paper over the firewood. He lit the paper. The firewood began to burn.

Sally and Homer took cooking supplies out of the plane to use to prepare a hot meal. Sally prepared grilled salmon and country-cut potatoes. She used a metal pot to warm frozen mixed vegetables which were packed with ice around them. She grilled some sourdough bread. She cut some fresh fruit such as apples, oranges and cantaloupe and mixed them together for dessert.

Once the meal was prepared Homer and Sally sat in folding chairs they took out of the small plane. They sat close to the campfire while they enjoyed their nutritious meal. After they ate their meal they cleaned up the cooking utensils and they placed all remaining food and cooking utensils in the airplane.

Homer and Sally decided to walk into Colville to look around and to buy some gasoline for their airplane. They locked the plane before heading for Colville. It took around forty-five minutes for the Applesteads to come into town. They walked down the main street. They had plastic, gasoline containers packed on their backs.

There were small shops and some cafes and one bank and some business buildings. Alaskans were walking in the streets. The sun was shining brightly. Some clouds were moving in the sky. Homer and Sally walked into a shop which provided clothing, household supplies and Alaskan artifacts. Homer saw a warm, Alaskan coat made with thick fur.

He tried on the fur coat. Sally tried on some black boots which could be used during cold, snowy weather. Homer decided to buy the warm, fur coat. Sally purchased the well made boots.

Sally and Homer browsed through more shops. They didn't buy anything else. Then they came to a cozy café. They walked in and sat at a comfortable booth. This café was decorated with pictures of Alaska. A server walked over to their booth and handed them menus. Sally and Homer studied the menus.

Homer decided to order a piece of apple pie and hot chocolate. Sally ordered a piece of berry pie and hot coffee. The server brought the pie and drinks to their table. The warm apple and berry pie was delicious. The hot chocolate and hot coffee also warmed Homer and Sally up. They sat in this Alaskan café and they felt comfortable.

The Applesteads finally left the Alaskan café. They walked further down the street to a gasoline station. They paid for 30 gallons of gasoline. They filled 5 gallons into each plastic container. They filled six containers. Once they had packed these containers on their backs they walked back to their campsite near their rented plane.

SIGNIFICANT MOMENTS

Homer filled the airplane gas tank with the 30 gallons of gasoline. Homer and Sally placed bedrolls in their tent. They went into their tent and got into their warm, dry bedrolls. It was still light outside. They zipped up the tent to keep wild animals out. They were tired and ready to sleep. During their resting time they heard some animal sounds.

The sound of wolves could be heard in the distance. Homer and Sally fell asleep. While they were sleeping some wolves came into their campsite looking for food. The fire was still flickering with fire and sparks. The wolves sniffed around the tent. They pawed the tent. However, the canvas tent was thick. They were unable to get into the tent. The pack of wolves finally left the campsite.

After 8 hours of rest it was still light out. Homer and Sally got up and came out of the tent. They rekindled the campfire. Sally fried some eggs and cut potatoes. She fried some bread. She poured orange juice from an orange bottle which was stored in ice to keep it cold.

Homer and Sally ate their warm breakfast and drank their orange juice. Sally prepared hot coffee for Homer and her to sip to keep alert and awake. The Applesteads packed all their belongings carefully in the plane. Homer put out the campfire very carefully.

It was time to continue the journey north in the small two passenger plane. Homer warmed up the plane and headed up into the sky northbound. He traveled to Barrow Point. The landscape below had no towns and no civilization. It was remote countryside. The Applesteads had traveled several hundred miles to reach Barrow Point on the north coast near the Arctic Ocean. There was no land below for hundreds of miles in the ocean.

Homer decided to turn the small plane around towards Alaska. He guided the plane over the Alaskan landscape and mountains to journey back to Nome on the central western coast. He hoped to have enough gas to make it home. He kept the plane above the clouds to avoid serious weather conditions. It took three and a half hours to travel back to Nome.

As Homer approached the Nome Airport the engine began to putter. The gas gauge indicated that the gas tank was empty.

Homer tried to glide the plane down on the runway. The plane was wobbly and had no more power. Homer finally managed to land the airplane on the runway. The wheels skidded onto the runway a number of times. Homer finally slowed the plane down and he gradually stopped the plane. Sally and he were safely on the ground again.

The Applesteads were grateful to be back on the ground again. They had traveled to a remote region in northern Alaska. They were glad to be back in Nome, where they lived. Their journey was over and they remained in Nome until they took another trip to another place.

FIFTY-EIGHT
RESOLVING ISSUES

Resolving issues is significant because problem solving is useful in resolving many issues. Individuals who go into politics must try to resolve important political issues. Psychiatrists and psychologists try to help their clients evaluate and face problems and emotional anxieties and stress in their lives. Businessmen, and business women use problem solving techniques to resolve problems and issues in their businesses.

Senators, Congressmen and Congresswomen take up political issues such as healthcare problems and needs to benefit many Americans in need of health insurance which will cover hospital bills, doctor visits, prescription costs and medical supplies. Every American needs healthcare benefits. Presently, many Americans do not have adequate health insurance benefits.

Senator Edward Kennedy was an American senator from Massachusetts for 47 years. He has been called the "lion" of the American Senate. Senator Kennedy has been working on healthcare issues, civil rights issues and other political issues during the 47 years he served in the American Senate. Senator Kennedy, who was called Teddy Kennedy, found ways to resolve health benefits and to promote equal rights, fair minimum wages and better working conditions in America, especially in Massachusetts. Teddy Kennedy helped pass over 1,000 bills while he served in the American Senate. He used effective, persuasive techniques when he communicated about significant issues.

Psychiatrists and psychologists use problem solving methods as mental therapy to help their clients face specific, emotional problems they have experienced in their lives. A patient is asked specific questions so that he or she can think about problems and traumatic experiences he or she has experienced during childhood and adult years. When a patient recalls traumatic experiences and reexamines why he or she felt severe fear, trauma, stress and anxiety, usually pain is released from their minds so he or she can accept and release the negative, emotional energy from their memories. Emotional traumas can be neutralized because the patient learns to understand and forgive traumatic experiences he or she experienced in the past.

Major problems must be faced in our lives. Problem solving techniques help us resolve these issues. First, we need to identify specific problems. Then we need to analyze and find solutions to remedy and solve the problems. Each major issue or problem can be resolved. We need to be consistent in our approach and acceptance of each problem and issue to succeed in overcoming major problems and issues.

FIFTY-NINE
FUTURE GENERATIONS

Future generations will be effected by the present and past generations. Past generations have also had some influence over the present generations. Each generation also develops new fashions and some different attitudes and beliefs. Each generation promotes certain changes.

Future generations may not have the same opportunities as we have presently if the world economy collapses. Future generations will need to be provided with higher education, cultural stimulation and a prosperous environment. If these opportunities are not available for future generations they will live by much lower standards and expectations.

Our present generation should pave the way in promoting better opportunities for future generations to improve in healthcare, sanitation and correction of air, water and earth pollution which will help to protect future generations. Use of government funds will effect future generations. If our American government continues to spend billions of dollars which causes extreme debts to be paid back it will be a burden for future generations.

The American government needs to balance our American economy. Debts should be paid off step by step. Our American government should provide a higher percentage of government tax money for education, health benefits and healthcare and for development of employment for many unemployed Americans. Extreme American debts may eventually cause American bankruptcy.

We need to protect future generations by improving our way of life. Today wealthy individuals should provide employment for needy people so they will have jobs to pay their bills. Employment opportunities should be increased for the percentage of people who are seeking employment today. More American money should be used to buy school books and other supplies. Classroom loads are increasing. Classrooms in elementary school shouldn't be over 25 students so teachers can provide more attention. Healthcare should be available for all Americans.

Future generations will need all the benefits that the present generation has today. In fact, future generations may expect to receive more benefits and financial protection. If the American government would stop spending nearly two-thirds of its budget on wars, weapons and other military expenses, and use those funds to help the American people, there would be adequate financing for education and healthcare. Helping to change these huge problems on Earth with taxpayers' money is an alternative to spending billions of dollars on unnecessary outer space projects. America's long history of giving taxpayers' money to aid foreign, corrupt dictators that eventually turn against America should never happen again. Furthermore, giving more money to Israel, in annual budgets, than the entire budget of California is neglecting the needs of the American people.

SIXTY
FANTASIES AND REALITIES

Fantasies are make believe tales, stories and dramas about fictional characters and make believe places. Real experiences and situations are nonfictional reports of true happenings.

Fairy tales, cartoons and fictional stories are presented in films, videos and DVD videotapes. Fantasies are acted out stage plays in the theaters and at community buildings. Walt Disney's MICKEY MOUSE AND MINNIE MOUSE cartoons are fictional. DONALD DUCK, ALICE IN WONDERLAND, CINDERELLA and SNOW WHITE AND THE SEVEN DWARFS are fantasy stories produced into cartoon movies.

Real events and happenings have taken place in THE DIARY OF ANNE FRANK, RED ROVER, THE GREATEST STORY EVER TOLD, BIOGRAPHY OF ABRAHAM LINCOLN, BIOGRAPHY OF GEORGE WASHINGTON, LEWIS AND CLARK EXPEDITION, THE LOUISIANA PURCHASE and many more factual stories, films and videos.

Realism is expressed in biographies, autobiographies, narratives and factual reports. Writers give details about peoples' lives, specific experiences, events and a variety of happenings. Realism awakens us to real experiences that we can identify with. We can learn how, what and why people behave a certain way. We find out about many experiences which really have taken place in peoples' lives. We can learn from their successes and failures how to live a better life.

SIXTY-ONE
DIAMOND MINES

Diamond mines exist in South Africa and in Ghana. Diamond miners use special digging equipment to dig out diamonds. Once diamonds are cut and polished miners take the diamonds to diamond dealers.

Diamond dealers determine the value of each diamond. The size and shape of a diamond is important to determine its value. Each diamond mine may have different quantities of uncut diamonds.

King Solomon's Mines have valuable diamonds. These mines have existed for many years and are well known. King Solomon lived in Africa. He acquired different mines and he collected a variety of precious gems, diamonds and gold.

Diamonds are made into rings, bracelets, anklets and necklaces. The diamonds are cut and shaped to the size needed for jewelry. Diamonds usually cost a lot of money. Some diamond rings and necklaces may cost thousands of dollars or more.

Diamond dealers generally purchase cut, polished diamonds from owners of diamond mines. Then the diamond dealers sell the diamonds to interested buyers. Diamond dealers can receive millions of dollars by selling valuable diamonds. They can become wealthy as diamond dealers.

SIXTY-TWO
HAPPENINGS

Happenings are experiences which take place in our lives. We may experience many adventures, novelties and traumas. How we are treated determines how we react to specific situations.

Shelley McCoy was an active, dynamic person who enjoyed many activities, events and adventures. She pursued school and community events. Every day Shelley attended after school sports. She played soccer, baseball and volleyball. She was very good as a baseball player, soccer player and volleyball player. She joined Girl Scouts and she went camping with other girl scouts.

Shelley McCoy was a leader at school. She organized committees in Social Studies and Science. She set goals and objectives for committees. Each committee gathered knowledge and information about a specific topic. Once the committees developed reports and visual materials about the topic, Shelley led the committees as they presented their topics before audiences.

Shelley continued with more activities and projects. She gathered gemstones and kept them in a glass case. She labeled them so observers could identify them by name.

SIGNIFICANT MOMENTS

Shelley participated in school plays. She was chosen as a main character in a school play entitled CINDERELLA. Shelley was chosen to be Cinderella. She attended drama rehearsals after school. She practiced her lines and stage movements. She learned to memorize all the lines.

A costume designer designed different dresses for the character of Cinderella. Shelley finally attended the final dress rehearsal. She continued to practice her lines as she projected her voice across the auditorium. The drama director gave specific directions how to speak and move on the stage.

That weekend CINDERELLA was performed on Friday night. Opening night was a challenging night. Shelley was nervous before the curtain went up. She hoped she would remember her lines. The drama coach gave everyone a pep talk before the performance.

The curtain went up. Shelley, who was acting as Cinderella, walked on stage and kindled a fireplace with wood. Cinderella was named after cinders. Her real name was Ella. Cinderella was expected to do all the work around the house and yard, plus cook all the meals for her stepmother and two stepsisters. So, Shelley, as Cinderella, began sweeping the floor. Then she dusted the shelves and furniture. Her stepmother came on stage and grumbled about her breakfast. She told Cinderella to go prepare her breakfast. Cinderella stepped over to a kitchen to the right side of the stage. She prepared eggs and bacon and made muffin dough to put in the oven.

Shelley continued to act out the part of Cinderella. The audience responded by clapping at the end of each major Act. CINDERELLA was enjoyed immensely by the appreciative audience. Shelley acted the part of Cinderella again on Saturday night and on the following weekend on Friday and Saturday night at the school auditorium. This stageplay was successful and appreciated by many people.

Shelley continued to be active at school and in her community in Santa Monica, California. She acted in more stage plays at her high school .

SIXTY-THREE
SOAP OPERAS

Soap operas are presented in series on television. DAYS OF OUR LIVES, THE YOUNG AND THE RESTLESS, AS THE WORLD TURNS and GENERAL HOSPITAL are soap operas which have been presented on television since the 1950s and 1960s.

A soap opera is a daily episode of dramatic moments and human behavior and reactions about personal problems and concerns. People such as housewives and retired women and men usually watch soap operas during the daytime. Viewers observe the emotional outbursts and problems in the soap operas.

Many problems are exposed in soap operas such as couples fighting, children running away from home, couples divorcing, conspiracies in businesses, robberies and even murders. Sibling rivalry and jealousy occurs in dramas. Each soap opera is a day by day continuing story. One problem leads to other problems step by step. The characters interact and relate closely in the dramas that unfold and develop.

Soap operas are designed to entertain people who have plenty of time to watch daily episodes. Each soap opera focuses on a specific theme with different characters and sets. Each theme develops over a long period of time. Soap operas are performed over a period of many years from Monday through Friday.

Some actors and actresses have performed in weekly soap operas for many years. They play the same character roles again and again. Soap operas will probably continue to be presented on television for many more years.

SIXTY-FOUR
WE CAN CHANGE

We tend to become set in our ways. We develop habits from childhood on. Then it seems difficult to break certain habits. We may develop habits such as chewing gum, nibbling our fingernails and eating junk food for snacks.

Children develop certain behavior patterns. Some children tend to be very aggressive on the playground. They get into fights and arguments. Other children are withdrawn and avoid playing with other children. Some children tend to tease others. Other children are considerate and nice to others.

We can learn to overcome bad habits such as overeating, smoking and drinking. Drinking sodas and eating food made of white flour and white sugar are bad habits as well. You can learn to eat nutritious foods such as raw fruits and vegetables. Organic, brown flour and fiber foods help to improve your health.

Speaking unkindly, falsely and unnecessarily is a bad habit. We can learn to control what we say and think about other people. We can speak with kindness and be gentle towards others. We should avoid cussing and using vulgar language. We can change our way of speaking in order to express positive thoughts to uplift others. What we say to others effects how they feel and creates a reaction, positive or negative in people's minds.

If you are a sloppy housekeeper you can learn to improve your housekeeping techniques. Dirty kitchen floors should be mopped. Carpets should be vacuumed regularly to take out dirt and dust. Dishes, pots and pans should be washed, dried and put away in kitchen cupboards. Beds should be kept clean with new sheets, pillowcases, fresh blankets and bedcovers. Beds should be kept well arranged and made to look attractive.

We should take a bath or shower regularly to keep our bodies clean. We should change our clothes regularly. We should comb our hair to look neat. We can learn to change our negative habits. We need to be willing to change to improve our lives.

SIXTY-FIVE
NEW PERSPECTIVES

Each person has the opportunity to develop new perspectives to become awakened and inspired. New perspectives help a person have a new lease on life. A person can broaden his or her horizons by creating goals and objectives which bring fulfillment and happiness.

New perspectives help promote personal incentives and self motivation. We can improve our lives by what opportunities we choose and live by. What may seem impossible is possible if we change our attitudes and opinions. A person who has positive viewpoints and accepts new possibilities and opportunities will be able to experience new and better awareness.

A person can attend college to major in topics such as Education, Social Science, Nursing, Liberal arts and many more topics to prepare for specific occupations. Better jobs are offered to more educated people. The economic status of a college graduate is better than a high school graduate.

Individuals who become teachers, architects, inventors, physicians, businessmen and businesswomen, college librarians, designers, administrators, economists and statisticians may receive much better annual income. They may enjoy their professional occupations. They usually develop new perspectives. Artists, writers and musicians are able to be creative as they express themselves.

New perspectives can be developed day by day, month by month and year by year. A person who creates goals and objectives to accomplish has a purpose for his or her life.

SIXTY-SIX
FACING DEATH

Everyone will have to face death. We are born and someday we will die. What is death? It is a time when one's soul and astral body, which are invisible, transcend to the invisible, astral plane or dimension.

Most people do not know what will happen at death. So, they are afraid to die because of fear of the unknown. A person does not remember why he or she was born. Life after death is mysterious. A soul finds out after death what will happen in the astral plane.

Some individuals, who have almost died, remember near death experiences. They describe going through a tunnel of light. They have seen beautiful colors in the tunnel. Loved ones greeted them and communicated with them. They felt love, joy and a sense of timelessness.

Near-death experiences can awaken certain souls about life after physical death. Pain and suffering is usually eliminated when a person leaves his or her physical body. There is a sense of relief and the soul continues with his or her consciousness on the astral plane.

Individuals who experience near-death experiences are told to come back into their bodies to continue their lives on Earth to fulfill their mission. They have a purpose for returning or they would have passed away.

If the physical body has become terminal with diseases or severe injuries it most likely will pass away. Their astral form still exists as they dwell on the astral plane. Death is like passing through a doorway to another room. Death is as natural as birth. We need to accept death as we accept birth.

SIXTY-SEVEN
INTROSPECTIONS

Deep introspections help a person look within for knowledge and wisdom. Through introspections a person learns to meditate and evaluate their actions and conscious thoughts. Introspection teaches an individual to understand life and to awaken to deeper truths and wisdom.

Philosophers and prophets have learned to think deeper and to meditate with depth and spiritual awareness. Prophets are capable of receiving higher consciousness and messages from Masters, God and Archangels. Prophets become world teachers. They guide masses of people.

Philosophers develop theories and philosophical viewpoints which they develop as a philosophy of life. Each philosophy has affected the way people think in a given generation.

Anyone can learn to develop introspections by going within to listen to the still small voice within. Just quiet your mind. Then allow deeper thoughts to flow through your mind.

Socrates was a Greek philosopher in ancient Athens. He was a deep thinker. He speculated about many issues and topics. He became a great philosopher. Moses, an ancient Jew, became the leader of the Jewish people. He guided the Jewish people and brought the Ten Commandments down from Mount Sinai.

SIGNIFICANT MOMENTS

David was another prophet who had faith in God. He allowed God to be first in his life. He became an important prophet in ancient times.

Spiritual leaders come to Earth with their introspections, prophecies and philosophies. We can learn from spiritual prophets and avatars how to live better lives.

SIXTY-EIGHT
EXPERIENCING FIRES

Fires can suddenly occur just about anywhere. Fires may be caused by lightning. Also, fires may be caused by people who are careless or who deliberately start fires.

If a fire starts near our dwelling place you should evacuate this neighborhood until the fire is under control and put out. Don't panic or lose control during a fire. Quickly take essentials with you if there is time. Travel far enough away from the fire.

If you are camping in the wilderness be aware of how to build a safe campfire. Take every step to put out your campfire properly. Campfires which are not properly extinguished may cause fires when you have left your campsite.

People who smoke should be careful to prevent their cigarettes from starting fires by accident. All cigarettes should be put out very carefully.

Fireplaces in homes should be safeguarded against dangerous fires which may cause a fire to start from sparks and burning ashes. Sparks and burning ashes may blow out of a fireplace which causes a fire to start. Your house may burn down because you don't have a protective screen over your hearth.

Fires can be prevented when people safeguard their homes and regional areas. We should not take for granted any open fire or fire in our homes or neighborhoods.

SIXTY-NINE
COUNT YOUR BLESSINGS

We should count our blessings everyday and night. Being grateful to God, our Divine Creator, is important. We should thank God for all the abundance we receive everyday.

Being thankful for what we have is a form of gratitude. Souls who pray to God are closer to God. They are appreciative and happier individuals, who generally help others.

Gratitude can go along way. When a person truly is thankful more abundance and happy times take place in his or her life. This person generally receives more blessings because he or she is grateful and receptive. So, be grateful for any and all blessings.

SEVENTY
USES OF RUBBER

Rubber was discovered over one hundred years ago in jungles where rubber trees grow. The rubber is tapped from trunks of rubber trees. The liquid rubber drips down into buckets. The rubber is taken to a rubber factory and processed into rubber.

Rubber is used for making different types of wheels and tires. Rubber is used to make many parts and household items. Even rubber dolls are made. Rubber is durable and generally lasting. It can be formed into many things for mankind to use.

Rubber tires have made it possible for cars, buses, airplanes and bicycles to operate because rubber tires are used on all vehicles except trains. Rubber is made into shower and sink mats, rubber nozzles and dispensers. Rubber surfing suits and diving suits are produced. Rubber door mats and car mats are produced.

Rubber is very useful to produce pipes and funnels for connecting gasoline and oil pumps in vehicles. Rubber coverings are used to insulate, protect and cover many objects. Rubber will continue to be produced to use in our technological age.